jersey angel

Also by Beth Ann Bauman

Rosie and Skate

Beautiful Girls

jersey angel

Beth Ann Bauman

WENDY
LAMB
BOOKS

Text copyright © 2012 by Beth Ann Bauman
Jacket art copyright © 2012 by Getty Images

Visit us on the Web! randomhouse.com/kids

Educators and librarians, for a variety of teaching
tools, visit us at randomhouse.com/teachers

Library of Congress Cataloging-in-Publication Data
Bauman, Beth Ann.
Jersey Angel / by Beth Ann Bauman. — 1st ed.
p.   cm.
Summary: Shapely seventeen-year-old Angel Cassonetti, who lives with her
younger siblings and single mother in a house at the Jersey Shore, finds it
hard to stay away from ex-boyfriend Joey Sardone.
ISBN 978-0-385-74020-3 (trade) — ISBN 978-0-385-90828-3 (lib. bdg.) —
ISBN 978-0-375-89900-3 (ebook) — ISBN 978-0-385-74021-0 (pbk.)
[1. Dating (Social customs)—Fiction.   2. Beaches—Fiction.   3. New
Jersey—Fiction.   4. Italian Americans—Fiction.]   I. Title.
PZ7.B32743Je 2012
[Fic]—dc23
2011030915

The text of this book is set in 12-point Goudy.

Printed in the United States of America

10 9 8 7 6 5 4 3 2 1

First Edition

for ml

summer

chapter 1

A whiff of seaweed blows in the window from across the bay, and the bed fills with sunlight. I reach for my sunglasses and have myself a long stretch. Maybe tonight will be a good time to see Joey, patch things up, and put a sweet ending on the day.

The screen door squeaks, feet dash up the stairs, and the kids charge into my room—Mossy with a meatball on a fork and Mimi sloshing Coke from a glass loaded with cubes, just the way I like it.

"Happy birthday!" Mimi shouts, plunking the wet glass on the dresser and jumping into bed with me.

Mossy hands me the fork. "I couldn't decide. Heated up or not."

"Cold is de-lish," I say, sitting up and taking a nibble. What service.

"Gimme." Mimi reaches for my sunglasses. She slips them on, curls on my pillow, and stares up at me. "Oh, I wish I was seventeen."

"You'll get there," I tell her. Mimi's short for Mimosa. She's ten. Mossy's eight. Mom was married to Tofu Bart when she had them, which should explain the names, and by the way, that's Mimosa as in the flowering tree, not the champagne cocktail.

Mossy hands me a leftover valentine with hearts and *Be Mine* in big loopy letters. On the back he's written *Angel, treat yourself to something special* and taped three dollar bills.

"Oh, my little man," I say, throwing an arm around him. He smiles shyly, dropping his eyes.

"I didn't make a card," Mimi says. "And I'm broke, but I have a cheer." She gets my shakers from the closet and stands at the foot of the bed in a purple bikini with a dirty white boa looped around her neck. She stamps her foot and waves the shakers.

> *"Angel is pretty!*
> *Angel is great!*
> *Angel is my sister*
> *And she goes on dates!*
> *Angel has a birthday*
> *And we'll have a cake—chocolate!*
> *Angel has boobs*
> *And they're not fake."*

She crashes to the floor in a split.

"Oh brother," Mossy says.

"Who has fake ones?" I say, chewing.

"Nefertiti's mom. She just got them. They're bazoom-bas." Mimi crawls back in bed. "So, you like it? On a scale from one to ten?"

"Loved it. Nine."

She stretches out on the bed and sighs. "If I was seventeen then I could do anything I want. Date boys and be mean to them when I feel like it and nice to them when I feel like it . . ."

"Why do you want to be mean to them?" I say.

She tilts her head. "Because!"

"I'm not mean to guys," I tell her. I take a sip of cold, fizzy Coke. Bliss.

"But you break up with Joey Sardone."

Mossy leans over and takes a bite of my meatball.

"Not because I'm mean. Because we need a little break now and then to spice things up."

She closes her eyes dramatically, and her cheeks grow rosy. "Oh, I want to spice things up!"

"Angel," Mom yells.

I lift the screen and hang out the window. She's standing in front of the house in a lime bikini top and jean shorts, holding a bucket and mop. She has a bandana tied around her hair.

"Happy birthday, kiddo." She shades her eyes. "How is it you're seventeen? That practically makes me an old goat."

"Hardly, Ma," I say.

She shrugs. "Gravity's getting the best of me." Here we go. The truth is, with her long, dark hair, dark eyes, and upturned mouth, she looks kind of like a forty-year-old Kim Kardashian. We all look like Mom, especially Mimi. "Okay, cake later. Now we work."

"I hate to clean!" Mimi yells, squeezing in next to me at the window.

"Me too!" Mossy whines.

"You think I like it?" Mom says. "We'll do it fast. Let's go. Mossy, where are my rubber gloves? Were you using them again for one of your experiments? Go find them."

He rolls off the bed and trudges downstairs.

We own three houses on the Jersey shore. Every summer we rent out two to some of the tourists who descend on our little barrier island like a stampede, which means we pile together under one roof. During the off-seasons, at least, we get to spread out and breathe. Mossy and Mimi live with Mom in the House, and I get my own place.

But now it's time to clear out. I grab a Walgreens bag and start unloading my drawers—bikinis, panties, bras, tanks, shorts, jeans. I throw it all in. I wad up my sheets and blanket and shove them in too.

Yup, we have three houses. My grandfather, Pop, bought the House years ago; then he won the Next-Door House in a poker game, or so the story goes, and old Mr. Zimmerman, who was a little in love with Mom, or a lot, apparently, left her the Corner House—*my* house. So three in a row, overlooking the bay. The moolah we make by renting has to last the rest of the year because Mom isn't cut out for nine-to-five, or so she says.

"Here. Help." I throw Mimi my duffel bag. "Take the closet."

She steps into my spiky sandals and admires herself. "Fierce."

I empty the medicine cabinet into a shopping bag—undereye concealer, eight tubes of lip gloss, hair gel, Tylenol, a couple of condom packets, and my birth control pills. In the bag it goes. I squeeze out toothpaste and brush my teeth as I chuck in shampoo, soap, three kinds of conditioner, a loofah, and a razor.

Mimi puts a sundress on over her bikini and swirls in front of the mirror. "Oh, I wish I was you . . . but still me."

"So basically you?" I spit in the sink and toss the toothbrush and paste into the bag.

"Basically." She teeters over in the sandals and looks up at me, her eyes all dark pupils. "Is it exciting to be you?"

I swish out my mouth with a handful of water. "What a question, Meems. Is it exciting to be *you*?"

"No," she whines. "I don't wear mascara. Or have a best friend like Inggy Olofsson. I basically hang out with Nefertiti. We just eat Popsicles and watch TV. I'm too pretty to be so boring." She lets out a tiny sigh and collapses to the closet floor.

"You're such a snot-nose," I tell her.

She tips her face up to me. "I can't help it."

"Sure you can. Hang in there." I lean over her and start dropping clothes off the hangers, some of them raining down on her head. "One day boys will come a-knocking and everything else too. And then there'll be no looking back."

"How exciting," she whispers.

Have I been excited in a while? Maybe not. Maybe I'm due.

"Girls," Mom calls, squeaking open the screen door. "Let's get a move on." She turns on the kitchen faucet and a blast of water hits the metal pail.

chapter 2

The mad cleaning spree lasted nearly all day, and we barely made a dent, which is what you can expect when half your crew is kids. And now all of us are under one roof, meaning me and Mimi are sharing a bedroom the size of a large closet, her on a cot smack up against my little bed. "Isn't this nice?" she said, reaching out across the sheets to hold my hand and chattering away into the night.

So that's why it's one a.m. and I'm wide awake sitting on the front porch in a bikini and shorts, digging my way through a bag of cheddar popcorn, when Mom's ex, Tofu Bart, walks up to the house, carrying a blender, of all things.

"I've been summoned," he says, holding up the appliance. "Now, if your mother asked for the electric mixer I wouldn't be worried, but the blender is bad news." With a deep sigh (poor TB is always sighing), he sits himself on the steps and reaches for the popcorn, though he's not one for the hydrogenated oils. "So spill the beans, kiddo. What does she want it for?"

"No idea. Icy drinks, maybe," I say, capturing my hair and clipping it with a barrette.

"See! I told you. Who's she having icy drinks with?"

Here we go. "Listen," I say, patting his knee. "Is this how you want to play it? All crazy and jealous? You'll become repellent. Think about it."

"Did she place a personal ad on Yahoo? She said she was going to."

"She might have," I half lie. Actually she did, and may she meet a good one quick! I don't tell him that, though. When my mother's between boyfriends the general mood around here is not so good.

"You know what I think? She met one she likes, and she's inviting him over for icy drinks!"

"Look at the moon, will you." Tonight it's golden red and impossibly full, high above us in the night sky.

"What a beauty." He sighs. "It fills me with awe."

"Me too," I say, nibbling on a kernel. "Me too." My hair pops out of the barrette in the humidity and mushrooms around me.

"I'll tell you what," he says, his hound dog eyes hanging heavy as he stares up at the sky. "Your mother is the one for me. My love is such that I'm willing to lend my blender, which she requested by email, mind you—didn't even bother to pick up the phone—so that she can have icy drinks with her new beau."

10

"Oh, Bart, you've got it bad. Have some more popcorn," I say, thrusting the bag at him. Poor TB really needs to get laid. What he fails to understand is that he doesn't have a hope in hell with Mom. She's always exasperated with him—rolling her eyes, swishing past him, calling him a dummy. And here he is still smitten, long after the divorce.

"Everyone asleep?" He looks back at the darkened house.

"All but me."

"Why not you?"

"I'm adjusting to life in the sardine can."

"You should like living with your family," TB says, shaking a finger at me. "You have too much freedom, missy. You're only seventeen."

"But an old and wise seventeen, wouldn't you say?"

He slides his eyes over to me. "How old were you when you got the patch from the pediatrician?"

"Thirteen. I had to quit. I smelled like an ashtray." That's ancient history, though, and I've been smoke-free for years. I jump up, go around back, get my bike, and walk it over the stones. "Well, I'll see you later." I hop on the seat.

"Where are you off to at this hour looking like that? Go put a shirt on. Pull back that crazy hair."

"Bart, really," I say nicely. "Don't you have enough to worry about?"

"Be careful, you." And there he sits, clutching his blender. Poor guy. "Hey," he yells as I pedal away. "Happy birthday!"

I ride past the Corner House—*my house!* A warm, sticky breeze stirs the air as I ride, but how nice it feels to be out in the night. I left three messages for Joey but he didn't call me back. I considered zipping over on my bike earlier tonight, but what I really wanted was for him to call.

Oh, the moon! The blazing moon. I stop and gaze at it and don't see Cork until he pulls up on his bike and squeals his brakes.

"Just look at that crazy moon," I say.

John Cork is one of those people who can smile with his mouth open and not look dumb. He's wearing a red bathing suit with GUARD written up the side, and his hair's in a salty do—dried slicked back after a swim in the ocean. He's already pretty tan, though it's only June.

"Just look at that crazy hair," he says, grabbing a handful of my long, curly mop, which grows to twice its usual size in this weather. "I could lose a hand in there."

"It's been known to happen."

He smiles, closed mouth this time. I've known Cork forever, and he's Inggy's boyfriend. Funny, they're both tall, blond, and skinny, though he's golden and she's pale as milk. "Why you up?" I ask.

He shrugs. "Twizzler?" He pulls a package from his back pocket.

"Sure." I take one, and we stand there yanking and chewing. "Sounds like Ing's having fun." Cork nods. She and I talked a couple of times today, while I vacuumed the floors and scrubbed the tub, but I wish she was here for my b-day. No matter, we'll celebrate soon.

Inggy and the O's are off on a round of college tours—this time Syracuse, Brown, and some other places I can't remember. She's headed somewhere good, while Cork and I are probably headed across the bridge to the community college. But Inggy has straight As and the O's have money, and Cork and I are on the lazy side with no moolah. I'm not complaining, really.

He gives my hair another tug.

"Watch it," I tease.

Then he leans in and gives me a kiss. A soft, slow one right on the lips.

"Hey there, mister . . . ," I say, a little surprised.

"Just a little mischief in the wee hours."

"You badass." I smile.

"Later, Cassonetti," he says, hopping on his bike.

I ride over to Joey Sardone's, a little lavender-colored house on the lagoon. The flower boxes under the front windows are overflowing with his mom's droopy purple and white pansies. *Water*, they scream, so I give them a drink with the garden hose and then walk around back to Joey's window and put my nose to the screen. "Hey, Joe, you awake?" Nothing. "Hey, Sardi."

His mattress creaks. "Angel?"

"Yeah, it's me." The lagoon laps against the dock in little licks. "Get up. For a minute."

"Man," he says, dragging himself to the window. He has a hairdo—it sticks up on one side and the front is mashed—and he's shirtless in boxer shorts. He raises the screen and frowns at me.

Let me tell you about Joey Sardone. He is something. He's tall and solid with smooth, hard muscles—a middle linebacker on the Ocean Heights High football team—and one of my most favorite people. He has dark hair and dark eyes, and when he lowers those dark eyes, which he does a lot because he's shy, he's all dark lashes. Sometimes I wonder if I love him. But if I have to wonder, then maybe not. I reach in and run my fingers along his bare side.

"What?" he says, flinching.

"Why so crabby? How about letting me in?"

"I don't think so."

"Come on." Usually he'd be popping out the screen and hauling me inside right about now.

"Look," he says finally, but he doesn't say anything else, so I lean against the house and wait. He lowers his eyes. "You want me. But you don't. Right or wrong?"

14

"It's not like that—"

"Right or wrong?" he cuts in.

"Listen—"

"Right or wrong?" he asks quietly.

I fold my arms, and he takes that as a "right." It's true; Joey and I break up a lot. I guess I like my freedom too much, but for me it's always only a time-out so I can feel like I'm back in my life with all the possibilities. I like possibilities. But after a time-out, I'm always ready to come back.

"The thing is," he goes on, "you don't really want to be my girlfriend, and now for once I don't want you to be."

"Really?"

"Really."

I search his face, but he's not giving anything away. "So who is she?"

He shakes his head. "There's no one."

"Seriously?"

But he won't answer.

"Well," I say, "how about one for the road?"

"I'm not going to be some horndog, Angel."

I reach in and slide my hand over his. "I don't mind a horndog."

"Nice. Real nice." He swats a mosquito.

"So this is *it*?"

He stares at me for what seems like a really long time until I start to squirm. I look up at the moon, glowing in the dark night like an eye watching us. The wind blows back my hair as if giving me a shove, but I can't seem to move away.

"I really like you, Angel," he says finally.

"I know."

"And happy birthday."

"I was wondering if you remembered."

"Why are you here?" He barely looks at me.

"I miss you, stupid."

"You'll stop missing me."

"I'm changing before your eyes," I say, meaning it. "Won't you kiss me?"

"Stop."

"One question. Is it no as in no way, or no as in not now?"

"Go. Don't beg," he says. "Sweet dreams," he adds with a poker face. He lowers the screen, and then the bed squeaks as he climbs in. And that's the end of that, apparently.

chapter 3

On day two of our mad cleaning spree we're all hot and in a mood. Plus Mom's on a diet and stops every hour to fire up the blender with a Slim-Fast shake or some fruit and ice concoction (Tofu Bart was wrong about the beau, but right about the icy drinks). "Do you think it's easy to get a date at my age?" she says, out of nowhere, holding down the blender lid while the ice whirls at top speed. Her face is sweaty and her hair's in a messy bun. "I'm eating rice cakes and drinking this junk all to lose a few damn pounds. Do you kids think a woman of a certain age has it easy in this life? Well, she does not!"

Here we go. "Knock it off, Ma," I say. Lots of guys think she's hot. The guy at the sub shop, for one. I remind her.

"The sandwich guy, for crying out loud? He has one foot in the grave and the other on a banana peel."

"The old lifeguard guy likes you too," Mimi says. "He told Nefertiti's dad that you have a sweet can. I heard it with my own ears."

"He's a whooping bore." She smiles, though, and I know without a doubt that my old lady likes hearing she has a sweet can, and honestly, who doesn't.

"Dad likes you," Mossy says, plopping his sweaty self on the couch.

"Off," she yells. "I just changed the slipcover. Your dad, pft!"

"What's wrong with our dad?" Mimi demands.

Mom pours her icy concoction into a glass and takes a grumpy slurp. "Not a thing, but he's not for me."

"You didn't think so when you married him," Mimi says.

"Well, I changed my mind, didn't I?"

"So listen." I peel off my rubber gloves. "Are we cleaning here or are we yakking—"

"You know what I think?" Mimi sloshes her sneaker through a wet puddle on the floor. "Rice cakes taste like Styrofoam." She does a wobbly pirouette.

"I wouldn't need to eat Styrofoam if I didn't have three snot-noses," Mom says. "Do you know what three pregnancies do to a waistline? Hand me that bucket."

"Not if you keep calling me a snot-nose." Mimi does a grand plié, waving her dust rag in the air.

"Now!" Mom yells.

So it's not a good time, obviously.

• • •

By day I'm a cleaning, scrubbing fool, and by night I'm living in the sardine can, where I lie on my narrow bed next to Mimi's cot, tossing and turning and flipping my pillow for the cool side until it's just no use; I can't sleep. Plus Inggy's still visiting schools, and worst of all, Joey isn't budging. I thought he'd come around. I really did. I want to give him the chance to miss me. Oh, I want him to miss me.

One night I'm lying in bed, the moon shining in my face, the smell of seaweed blowing in the window, which I'm convinced is some kind of perverted aphrodisiac, and try though I might not to, I rise from the top sheet and put on a string bikini and shorts, let down the crazy hair and give it a shake, spritz myself with some jasmine body mist, and slick on the lip gloss. Then, like a horndog, I get on my bike and head over to Joey's.

So basically, standing outside his window becomes a regular late-night activity for me. Alongside the Sardones' shed are crab nets, a rusted outboard motor, and a wobbly barstool. I move the stool over to the window for our meetings—Joey yawning on one side of the window and me perched on the stool on the other. And it goes something like this:

"You again?"

"Me again."

"Why are you bugging me?"

"I kind of think if I was truly bugging you, you wouldn't come to the window."

"I'm kinda wondering when you're gonna run out of gas."

And not once does he invite me inside.

We're cleaning in the Next-Door House and I send Mimi upstairs to scrub the toilet. When I check on her, she's brushing sparkly purple eye shadow across her lids from a compact she found behind the bowl.

"How do I look?" she asks, fluttering her eyes.

"You want to turn into a slut?"

"No."

"Then clean up your act." I swipe at her face with the bottom of my tank top.

"Get off!" she yells, squirming free and jumping on the toilet seat. "Now, I want your opinion. On a scale of one to ten, how obnoxious am I? Because Nefertiti says an eight, but Mossy only says seven."

"Somewhere right around there." I take the sparkle shadow out of her little paw, dust my lids, and blink into the mirror.

"Pretty!" She jumps off the bowl and hugs me. "Were you ever obnoxious like me?" She tilts up her face.

"Do you realize, Meems," I say, rapping on her skull,

"that the bennies arrive in *two days*?" Bennies are the tourists (and our renters) who clog up the island all summer long. They're called bennies because they're here for the benefits—summer sun, warm water, the boardwalk—and they take over the place, causing traffic jams and long lines in the A & P, Fat Sal's pizza, the sub shop, and every store and restaurant along the strip. Worse, they rise bright and early and park themselves on the best spots on the beach. Plus they're a sight to behold with their zinc oxide noses and peeling sunburns. Picture it: a typical benny takes a wheelie cart up to the beach loaded down with chairs, umbrellas, inner tubes, and Boogie boards, and over their benny shoulders they sling mambo-sized beach bags overflowing with Fritos, towels, thermoses, sunblock. . . .

I blend in the shadow with my fingers and hand Mimi the toilet brush. "Bennies!"

"The bennies can suck it!" She plunges the brush into the bowl and slops water over the side.

True, but bennies are how we get our moolah. Mom has a mishmash of jobs that don't bring in much cash.

Now, Mossy's a different story. The kid works. He doesn't like it one bit, but he parks himself on a step stool at the kitchen sink and plunges his arms into the soapy water, washing every dusty dish, pot, and pan until his fingers are pruny. I come up behind him and dig my chin into the top of his hot, sweaty head. "How's it going, little man?"

"No talking," he snaps.

• • •

Finally we finish. The houses are gleaming, and the first bennies pull up to the Corner House in an SUV loaded with suitcases. The dad benny steps out of the car and stands with his hands on his hips, breathing in the sea air. "Just look at him. The fatso," Mimi whispers, standing next to me on the porch of the House. Mom flies out the door and comes back, waving a rent check in the air. And suddenly I'm feeling pretty darn good.

No matter that I'm living in the sardine can and that someone's always in the bathroom when I need to get in there. No matter that Mimi is my chatterbox roommate. No matter that bennies walk among us. Summer has officially started, and all these long, sweet days are before us.

Inggy will come back soon and Joey will budge. Summer has begun, and I am filled with hope.

"You gotta stop," Joey says, coming over to the window.

"Look, I don't want to come in," I lie.

He lowers his eyes. "Well, I'm not inviting you."

"I know." A cricket chirps nearby, and it's a warm, lush, star-filled night. I lug over the wobbly barstool and take a seat. "Did I wake you?"

"Not really."

"So what's new with you, Joe? Tell me something."

He rubs his face. "You're giving me assignments now?"

"I miss talking. I miss everything else, but I really miss talking to you. Tell me what's new. I have no idea."

He drags his finger against the screen and thinks for a minute. "I'm really into fancy cheese."

"Fancy cheese?"

"You asked."

"Tell me."

"My cousin Dom's working in this new deli in the Heights. Kind of upscale, and I went to a cheese tasting last week and had gruyère and stilton."

"I wonder if I've ever had fancy cheese."

He shrugs. "You probably have a refrigerator full of the usual suspects: American, swiss, provolone, mozzarella, ricotta . . ."

"Exactly. You haven't become some cheese snob, have you? American's okay for like a grilled cheese, right?"

"Listen. I can now tell you without a doubt that American has no excuse for existing."

"Mozzarella?"

"No soul. Mozzarella has no soul."

I fake a gasp. "What kind of Italian are you, Joey Sardone?"

"The fancy-cheese-eating kind."

"I had no idea."

"And my mom doesn't want to know about fancy cheese. So I have to hoof over to the deli to buy my own. You've never had stilton?"

I shake my head.

"Just wait." And for the first time that night he smiles at me.

He disappears, and in the dark of his room I can make out his rumpled blanket and his lone pillow and the fan ruffling the edge of his sheet. I know that pillow—too flat—but how I'd like to lay my head on it now.

He comes back with a wedge of stilton on a cutting board and lifts the screen and makes a table out of the sill. He serves me a slice on the edge of the knife.

"Wow," I say.

"Yeah."

"Wow," I say again.

"I know." We laugh with glee.

I pop another piece in my mouth. "Zingy for sure. I bet we stink." I breathe on him.

"Well, I'm not kissing anyone," he says.

"I guess I'm not either." I try to catch his eye, but he won't look at me. "You know, I wouldn't mind some horndog with my cheese."

He tries hard not to smile, but it doesn't exactly work, and a slow one creeps onto his face before he can pull it back in. "See, I don't like that," he finally says with a straight face. "And I'm going to tell you why."

"I'm all ears."

"I don't want to sleep around. I want to sleep with my *girlfriend*."

"What? You're a good Catholic now?"

He shakes his head. "I don't even go to Mass anymore, so don't give me that." He thumps his chest. "I'm speaking from here, from what I know to be right."

"Um, what about Alyssa?" I remind him.

"Live and learn, Angel. Live and learn."

I broke up with Joe in the spring and he briefly hooked up with Alyssa, a pretty, tiny girl on the cheerleading squad who we always put on top of the pyramid when we're ambitious enough to make one. Mostly we're too lazy, but when we do, Alyssa climbs up and stands shakily with one foot on my back and the other on Carmella's. And before she pitches forward into a perfect somersault she always makes the sign of the cross. Mostly she gets caught at the bottom. So Joey had a fling with her while I was having my own adventures; then Joey and I missed each other too much and patched things up.

"Well," I say, smoothing down my hair. "For the record, I like sleeping with you, and I'm not going to feel bad about it."

"But why don't you want to *be* with me?" he asks, putting down the knife. "I don't understand you. Why don't you want a boyfriend?"

"But I do," I say quietly.

"Until you don't. I don't understand you at all."

"You're one of my favorite people."

"That's no help." And all our cheese happiness is suddenly gone.

He won't look at me as we finish off the wedge of stilton. I see the price on the plastic—$7.99 for a dinky square that's about four bites' worth. "I thought you were saving for a car," I say.

"I am, but now that I know about fancy cheese . . . what can I do?"

"Then there's the cracker issue," I joke. "If you're going to have fancy cheese you can't slap it on some cheapo cracker. So that means fancy crackers, right?"

But he's not listening to me. He picks up the cutting board and starts to lower the screen.

"Hey, I can take a hint," I say. "And for the record, you are an excellent boyfriend."

"Don't kiss my ass, all right?"

chapter 4

"Angel, how about a grilled soy cheese?" TB says. It's his night to take the kids, but here he is, hovering over our stove with a spatula.

"Have you ever known me to eat a grilled soy?" I say.

"It's nice with tomato, but suit yourself. So where is that mother of yours?" His cheeks are flushed and he is clearly a man with hope in his heart, even if he is barking up the wrong tree.

"Out and about." I reach for a handful of grapes. Here we go. We're about thirty seconds from him grilling me about her online adventures, when the screen door creaks open and Mom pads in, in her flip-flops with cotton between her freshly painted pink toenails.

"Hello there." TB flips the sandwich in the skillet.

"Oh, it's you. Are you messing up my kitchen?"

"I'm feeding the kids. You want one?"

"Move it," she says, sliding around him to get in a

drawer. "And for the tenth time, I'm on a diet. Do you ever listen to what I say?"

Well, that's my cue, and I am outta there. In the backyard, Mimi comes charging up to me in a polka-dotted bikini.

"What did one saggy tit say to the other saggy tit?"

"I have no clue."

"If we don't get some support soon, people will think we're nuts."

I giggle.

"I don't get it," she says. "Mossy gets it but he won't explain."

"I didn't say I get it or not," he says.

"Liar!" she yells.

To stop the titty talk, Mossy comes after us with the hose and sprays our legs. He chases us down the length of the yards as we duck under the rows of benny beach towels flapping on the clotheslines. At the Corner House, I stop and peer in the back door, wanting to get a good look at who's living in my house.

"Nosy!" Mimi says.

"Shush," I say. Just then Bart calls the kids in for their sandwiches and they take off. What can I say—the tofu gene is in their blood.

The house is empty, as far as I can tell, so I slip inside, where it feels and smells like a completely different place. Funny how the bennies can completely make a house a home, even when they're here for only a week. Strewn around the kitchen are some mangoes, *Sun and Sand: A Complete Guide to the Jersey Shore* (the benny bible), a neon Frisbee, hot dog buns, a package of Dentyne, and bottles of root beer. I take a handful of barbecue chips from a bag on the counter and head up to the roof deck, where I sprawl out on the chaise, half hidden by the ficus in case I have to make a quick escape. I love this spot. There's a nice breeze coming off the bay, and the late-afternoon sun blazes low in the sky.

The chaise—fifteen bucks at a yard sale—has a leopard print and it's threadbare in places, but it's awfully comfy. With my late nights these days, I yawn and feel myself drifting off. Luckily I hear the squeaky wheels of a benny cart coming down the street. The cart is pushed by a belea- guered benny guy flanked on one side by the wife, I'm guessing, in a visor, bathing suit, socks, and sneakers, and on the other side by two whining kids, pink as raw meat. I'm pretty sure they're my bennies, so I flee out the back.

Since TB's still at the house, I ride over to my dad's marina, where I have a part-time job pumping gas, which is kind of the ideal job. I love the smell of gasoline and I get to be outside, and there are lulls when there's no boat traffic, so I can sprawl out on the dock with a magazine or hang out with the marina dog, a two-hundred-pound En- glish bull mastiff named Joop (short for Jupiter).

Dad's sitting at his messy desk surrounded by mounds of

paper. He's cute, my dad. When he started going bald in the worst way—bald top, ring of hair around the sides—he smartly shaved it all off. He's got a goatee and nice dark eyes, gentle eyes. "Hey, sweetheart." He looks up at me. "You're not on the schedule, are you?"

"Just visiting. I thought we could get something to eat." I kind of hope we can do something—the two of us— which never happens, but I'll settle for an invite to his house.

"Aw, Angel, both kids are sick. They were throwing up last night."

"Yeah? Okay." As if I haven't been around a sick kid.

"Here, sit a minute," he says, jumping up and moving papers from the plastic chair. My dad's basically a nice guy, but he's remarried, with two little girls, and the truth is I don't quite fit in. I mean, he's my dad and he loves me, but Ginger, the wife, doesn't exactly like the fact of me. Oh, she's nice enough, but it's like I'm a guest in that house. I mean, I can't hang out, plop on the couch, pour myself a soda. She hovers, all polite. Wouldn't you think politeness like that would wear off, say, after a couple of weeks? It's been years. A real cool cucumber, she is. And my dad is overworked. He made some bad financial deal, and the poor guy has debt up the wazoo.

So I hang out and we talk, during which time Ginger calls twice. When Dad gets up to leave for the day, he jingles his car keys and says, "Look, it's okay about the kids. Why don't you come over for dinner."

"You sure?"

"Well . . ." He sighs.

"Next time," I say, quick. All he needed to say was *yes, come* and I would have.

As I'm leaving, Rob, who works in the yard, asks me if I want to put in a couple of hours, because the marina's gotten busy. So I pump gas, and he tosses me a few White Castle burgers from a gigantic bag. Joop hangs out with me on the dock as the boats pull in and out. He's a gentle giant, a real lovey boy. I lie in front of him and take his big old head in my hands and look into his soulful eyes.

"How's it going, Joopy boy?" He licks me. "I have boy trouble, if you can believe it," I tell him. "But I'm practicing the art of patience. You know about patience, don't you?" He yawns and settles his head between his paws.

Then a very cute guy who graduated a few years ago pulls up in a Boston Whaler and swings himself onto the dock. "Long time no see." He has shaggy blond hair and his madras shorts hang low, showing his briefs.

"Hey there." I hand him the pump.

"When am I gonna take you for a ride?"

"I'm ready whenever," I tell him with a smile.

"So come on."

"As you can see, I'm working."

"Next time."

As the sun sets and the marina quiets down, I decide to visit Joey on the boardwalk, where he works his dad's stand.

I spy on him from the Kohr's stand. "Come on over. Check it out. A prize every time," he calls to people strolling along with their slices and cones. What is his life like these days? I know he's working a lot, and football practice starts in late July. After a long night at the stand he probably goes home and makes himself comfy on the couch with a nice plate of fancy cheese and maybe thinks about finding himself a girlfriend. I wonder. How much does he really miss me? Does he want to give it another go? Underneath it all I think he does. The prospect of a ride with the very cute guy with the madras shorts just isn't as appealing to me as hanging out on Joey's couch with a plate of cheese, fancy or not.

Not much action tonight at the water balloon stand. Joey sits on a stool, props his feet up on the ledge, and yawns. Just then Carmella walks over and starts talking. She tilts her head, tosses her long, glossy hair, and laughs. She's a big flirt, a little bit stuck up too, but we're friends. Cheerleaders. She's all right. She has the most amazing bag. At the right moment she can whip out just what you need—a tampon, a spritz of perfume, a string of dental floss, a chocolate Kiss, a Band-Aid, a dousing of Off.

32

So I bide my time and visit my friend Vic, who's working the Ferris wheel. We were never an item, but we fool around now and then. I sit with him for a while as the bennies climb in and out of the cars. We play a few rounds of rummy and yak. When I know Joe will be getting ready to close up, I head back.

"Hey there," I say, walking slowly over to the stand.

"Well, look who it is." Joey glances at me. A couple of stuffed Bart Simpsons have tipped over on the shelf, and he sets them neatly in a row.

"You want to hang out?" I say.

"Hang out?"

"Yeah." I pick up a leaky gun and point it at a clown head. Joey flips the switch, and I aim the stream of water into the mouth, making the blue balloon grow bigger and bigger until it bursts with a satisfying pop. "Let's hang out on the beach."

He looks down to the water, deep in thought. "Yeah, okay," he says finally, taking a five-dollar bill out of his pocket. "Why don't you go buy us zeppoles while I finish closing down. I'm kind of hungry."

"No cheese?"

"Maybe later."

"All right."

I hurry off to the zeppole stand, which is a ways down the boardwalk, where I get us two hot zeppoles right out of the deep fryer and sprinkled with powdered sugar. Then I hurry back, and what do I find? The stand is closed up, the gate is lowered and locked, and Joey's nowhere in sight. Ditched. Even so, I walk down to the beach on the minuscule chance that he's sitting on the sand, waiting for me, which of course he isn't.

How do you like that. I mean, *damn*. I park myself on the sand and eat my zeppole, licking my fingers clean of grease and sugar. This isn't like him. Not at all. Where'd he go, my Joey? The guy who gives me a ride on his handlebars, calls me to say good night, whispers into my hair when he tells me I'm pretty, trails his fingers down my bare back when we're in bed?

I ride over to his place and park myself outside his window. "So what do you have to say for yourself?" But there's no answer, and as my eyes adjust to the dark inside I can see his bed's empty. Double ditched. I pry open the screen and toss the powdery zeppole onto his rumpled sheets. "Have that with your cheese."

How I miss Inggy. On my way home, I ride by her place, and to my surprise the Olofsson car is in the drive, and Ing's window is lit. I climb the sycamore—an easy climb—up to the roof deck and see her hunched over her desk, tapping her lip. I scramble through the window.

"Hey, you!" she says, spinning around in her seat. "We're back early. I called you a couple of times from the car, then called the House and Meems said you were nowhere to be found."

"I'm found!" I say happily, reaching for my phone. Forgot to charge it. We hug. I kick off my flip-flops and lie across one of her twin beds, and she lies across the other, facing me.

Let me tell you about Inggy: the O's moved from Sweden to the island when we were in second grade. There was Inggy, the color of milk, with long white ponytails jutting out over her ears and spilling down her arms. She was the size of a toothpick, and she'd brought some kind of smelly fish in her lunch box. And she came right up to me at the lunch table, big blue eyes, her face merry. "I can sit here?"

"Well, okay," I said, making room. She squeezed in next to me, all smiles, and tucked into her smelly Swedish lunch was a good old-fashioned American donut, which she whipped out proudly for me to see. She took a big powdery bite and thrust it at me, so I took a bite too. We were instant friends, little Inggy Olofsson and me. Who would have thought she'd grow so tall and spindly. At five eleven, she's the boniest and most glamorous person I know. Her white hair falls down her back and all summer long she's slathered in 45 sunblock and wears enormous sunglasses that make her look like some beautiful bug. Tonight she's wearing a red bandana skullcap and has a pencil tucked behind her ear.

"What were you furiously scribbling over there?" I ask.

"The dreaded personal essay. You're supposed to make yourself shine. Show how noble you are. What an asset you are to the community and all that. So I'm reading all these samples and they're *such* crap." She folds her pillow in half and rests her head on it. "You know, stuff like befriending some old hag and shopping for her Depends. Loathsome, ass-kissing stuff." Ing, I should mention, loves the word *loathsome*. "Total disingenuous bullshit." She pulls the pencil from behind her ear and waves it at me. "I refuse to partake."

"Good," I say.

"Thanks, my friend."

"Write about our parties in the benny houses."

"Ha!"

Back in the winters in seventh and eighth grades we'd break into some summer bungalow and bring space heaters and candles, and we'd have small parties of the vodka and orange juice and Ouija board variety. After some rounds with the Ouija, couples would pair off and make out in the bedrooms. I made out with lots of boys in those benny bedrooms, shivering on the cold mattresses, our cold lips pressed together. Inggy and Cork were a couple even back then, so they only locked lips with each other.

Anyway, Inggy was very decent about our break-ins. She once replaced a tablecloth that one of us accidentally scorched with a cigarette. Another time she insisted we

36

return the next day to scrub a bathroom after one of our moron friends blew chunks.

"Look," I say. "Think of the angles. You've got resourcefulness, responsibility . . ."

"There's my essay," she jokes.

"Bullshit-free."

She sits up and smiles at me. "I'm glad to be home."

"I'm glad you're home."

"And happy birthday! Let's celebrate."

"How about some hors d'oeuvres and cocktails?" I say.

Inggy rubs her hands together and springs off the bed.

We head down to the clean white kitchen, where Mrs. O is padding around in a baggy summer nightgown. "Angel, sweetie." She smells fresh from the shower, soap and cold cream. "Tell me everything," she says, plopping into a chair. She has chin-length blond hair and heavy bangs, like a doll's, and two front teeth that overlap. But she has great bones and eyes—that's where Inggy gets her good looks.

So I tell her about our renters. She likes hearing their antics.

"Lookie," Inggy says, digging through the freezer. She holds up a box of mini hot dogs wrapped in dough.

"Excellent," I say. We love pigs in a blanket.

"Don't forget a birthday toast." Mrs. O winks. Swedes like to drink.

"Yup." Inggy pulls out a bottle of green apple martini mix and starts making a batch. Mrs. O hands me a little package with a bow. Inside is a three-pack of nail polish in amazing blues and purples.

"I bought one for me too." Mrs. O laughs. "I want blue toes!"

"She does!" Inggy brings over the cocktails. We clink glasses, and Inggy hands me a bow-topped present too: big hoop earrings and a three-pack of lip gloss in sangria, watermelon, and guava-gold.

Yawning, Mrs. O kisses us and floats away, carrying her cocktail upstairs. Ing tops off our glasses while I grab ketchup, mustard, and a half container of double fudge icing from the fridge.

We clink glasses again.

"To summer," I say.

"To summer," she says. "To senior year."

I take a long sip. "Nice and sour. So tell me what's happening."

She tells me about the schools and campuses and assorted dorms, including a story about a resident mouse named Herman on one of the floors that the girls refuse to kill. I fill her in on my boring days of cleaning and my nightly visits to Joey. "Might be a phase," I say. "But I don't know. . . . He's just not budging."

"He'll budge."

"I don't know. . . ." I dip a spoon into the icing and lick

it clean. "I have a bad feeling this time, and I almost never do. Not with Joey."

"You've got to stop dumping him."

"The thing is, Ing, most guys would love a time-out every now and then."

"He's not a time-out kind of guy. Quit dumping his behind."

I get up and open the toaster oven. The puff pastry is steaming hot and the juicy smell of hot dog fills the room. I put on an oven mitt and place the sizzling tray on a cutting board. "Dig in."

"Another toast," Inggy says, leaning toward me. "A close call . . . but the little pink stick said negative."

"Oh no."

"Oh yes."

"How late were you?"

"Well, I should have gotten it this morning."

"*What?*" I cry.

She gives me a withering look. That's another word she likes—*withering*. "I happen to be like clockwork, so wipe that smirk off your face. It was due early this morning and morning came and went, then afternoon, then night. As soon as we pulled in the driveway I was in a complete panic, so I hopped on my bike, went to CVS, and bought two tests—you know, the early-response kind. Both negative. And then twenty minutes later it started."

"I've got news for you, dodo. That's not late."

"For *me* it is."

I shake my head and laugh. "You're cuckoo. You know that, right?"

Inggy squirts mustard over one of the little dogs and pops it in her mouth. "God," she says with her mouth full. "I wish I could take the pill. I hate the loathsome paraphernalia." She got bad headaches from the pill, though, so she and Cork switch off with condoms and a diaphragm. The first time she used the loathsome diaphragm, she couldn't get it out and she called me one afternoon, crying from the bathroom. "It's stuck! I can't reach it!"

"Relax," I told her.

"It should come with a handle or a plunger or something," she sobbed. "Help me!"

"You're all worked up and you're probably, like, sucking it in."

"Will you come over and try to get it out?"

"Me? Can't you get Cork to do it?"

"He's out back taking a nap."

"Wake up his lazy ass and tell him to get in there and get it." Luckily they were able to fish it out. Remembering this gets me to thinking about Joey. If I had a diaphragm and it got sucked up in there, I know in a second he'd help me fish it out. I wouldn't have to ask twice. And of course, this makes me feel really lousy, things being as they are.

"Back in a sec." Ing runs upstairs and a minute later comes flying down with the bathroom garbage. "The evidence must be disposed of." She shows me the negative signs on the sticks, then ties up the bag.

"Phew. What a close call," I try to say with a straight face.

"Shut up." She pokes me in the side with a bony elbow.

We finish our drinks, and Inggy dips a finger in the icing and licks it, her forehead sweaty and glistening. "Tipsy?"

"A little." The ceiling fan stirs the warm air.

She looks down at the tied-up bathroom garbage bag. "Come on. Let's get rid of this."

We walk a block to the ocean. At two in the morning, most of the houses are dark and quiet. Inggy tosses the bag into a garbage can by the beach entrance. "Adios."

"Come on," I say. We walk to the water's edge, where there's a breeze.

"Oh, nice," Inggy says, flapping her arms.

I let the cool water rush over my feet and splash up my legs.

"I've been thinking about next year," she says, swirling her foot through the wet sand. "I have this little fantasy, so hear me out. You'll probably go to Ocean Community, right? So I'm thinking this: *instead*, you and Cork come with me wherever I go. There's bound to be a nearby community college, and we could all rent a house maybe—"

"You have *got* to be kidding me!" I cry. "Yeah, Inggy goes to Syracuse, and when she trots off to some party she brings her tag-along doofus friends who go to the community college down the street." Inggy gives me another withering look. "Think about it," I say. "God, Ing!"

She runs her foot through the wet sand. "I just want to figure out a way for all of us to be together."

"Yeah, I know."

"And you're not a doofus."

"Hey, thanks."

As the water washes over my feet, I look around at the dark, empty beach and peel off my tank. "Let's go in."

"All right."

We run up to the dry sand and strip down to our underwear. "What the hell," I say, wriggling out of that too. Inggy takes a quick look around before flinging off her bra and pushing down her panties. Then we rush at the waves.

I glance at her, the shocking whiteness of her, all long, skinny arms and legs, not an ounce of fat, her little boobs. She dives under a breaker, and when she surfaces, her white, wet hair is plastered to her. It's low tide, so we swim out a ways, and she floats on her back, spitting a stream of water into the air.

"Angel, you've got some great boobs."

"Thanks, I like them," I say, looking down. They're full and firm, perfect handfuls.

She swims over. "Oh, I wish I had bigger boobs. Let me touch them."

"Get out!"

"Come on," she says, splashing me. "I've never felt big ones. Give me a thrill."

So I fall back into the waves and let her feel me up. "They are simply amazing." She giggles.

I reach out and touch her little boob, a booblet. "Don't!" She slips away, giggling some more. "God, I'm so flat!"

"I don't know, Ing. I think you got a mouthful there." And we both flop back into the water, laughing. I tip my head and gulp in the dark, starry sky. "Hey, what's going to happen to us?" I say.

"What do you mean?"

"Don't you wish we could just hang out . . . be seventeen for a few years?" I think about Joey, this summer that's about to bloom, senior year . . . and then it's like I can't see any further.

"We'll have a good year, Angel."

"Oh, I know." But I wish she knew what I meant.

chapter 5

I've never had trouble with guys; maybe it's because I really like them. I'm driven to put myself right in their paths— like the cartoon mouse that's roused by a delicious smell and lifts its nose in the air and follows the scent. That's me. But I also don't get hung up on them. If I put myself in a guy's way and he doesn't do anything, well, later for him.

But with Joey things have always been a little bit different. He's someone I've known all my life but never really knew. Then in eighth grade he shot up and got cute, his shy, dark eyes glancing out at the world, and girls started noticing him. At the only benny break-in party he ever came to, we wound up together in a bedroom. He lay on his back on the benny mattress with his hands folded behind his head, trying to look all cozy, but honestly the guy was stiff as a board. I snuggled up to him and said, "So? You want to make out?"

"Shouldn't we talk first?"

"Okay then." I flipped over on my stomach.

"You do the algebra homework?"

"Not yet."

"I did most of it. The last two were hard. I'll take another look tomorrow."

"That's enough talking," I whispered, moving in for a kiss. And he gave me a dry, cold peck on the lips.

"I don't want to make out with every girl here."

"You don't have to, dummy," I said, trying to move in again.

"I know who I don't want to make out with."

"But do you want to make out with *me?*"

"I think so."

"You think so?"

Then he got quiet for a minute. "We were both starfish in that play. In third grade."

I flopped on my back with a sigh and stared up at the dark ceiling. "I was supposed to be a jellyfish but Franny James got sick, so yeah, I substituted as a starfish."

"*Sea Creatures on Parade,*" he said.

"Huh?"

"That was the name of the play."

"Look, Sherry and Leo are next. So it's now or—"

"All right, all right," he said, as if I'd asked him to hop into the dentist's chair. He leaned toward me, and just as his lips reached mine—

"Time's up," Sherry called, and she and Leo bounded into the room. Joey never came to another break-in party after that one, but we did talk from time to time over the next couple of years. And sometimes I would see this look in his eye and think *Here it begins*, which is what I always think when I first get together with a guy. But then, zip. He wouldn't do anything. So I had a lot of boyfriends, and quite honestly, I didn't think much about Joey Sardone.

Then last year I was standing at my locker, wiping my forehead with an acne pad and considering my afternoon options, when he came up and said, "Hey, Angel."

"Hello there, Joey Sardone."

He looked in my locker at the mess of books, papers, and candy wrappers. "You're a slob."

"True."

"Want to get a snow cone?"

A snow cone! I burst out laughing. A snow cone. It was like one of those old-fashioned movies where the guy says to the gal, *Let's have a root beer float*. But I'm a friendly girl, so I said, "I'd love a snow cone." I gathered my stuff and we got on the bus and stopped off in the Heights. It was a beautiful spring day, the kind with a hint of summer in it, the kind that makes you wish you were wearing flip-flops. We walked along the boardwalk, where rows of seagulls watched us from the railings, and off we headed to the Kohr's stand.

He took out his wallet. "You want ice cream instead? 'Cause apparently a snow cone is hilarious."

"But I would love a cherry snow cone." I sidled up next to him.

We sat ourselves on a bench with our snow cones—his lips turning blue with each bite—and we talked into the afternoon. When the breeze kicked up and my crazy hair blew all around, I gathered it off my face and tied it up with an elastic. Watching me, he said, "I love the way you look."

I smiled.

"You have a calm face, Angel."

"Calm?" Here I was thinking a *pretty* or *sexy* was coming my way.

He nodded and looked out at the waves, and his face lit with some happy, secret thought. "It's like . . . like you're waiting for a bus and you're sure it will come."

Now, I've been told all the usual things by a boy who's into me. But this bus business . . . who knew. Not that I minded, exactly. When I told Inggy later, she let loose a laugh, saying, "He's so weird and great. I love it."

That night I took a look at myself in the mirror, turning my head this way and that. I just didn't see the connection between my face and an oncoming bus, though in theory I thought I knew what he meant; I'm the anti–Chicken Little. Mossy was crazy for that story when he was little. "Goosey Loosey," he'd whisper over and over again. Anyway, I'm not a the-sky-is-falling type. I expect, in fact, that the sky will remain where it is, which makes me an optimist, which was probably Joey's point.

So that was our beginning. Joey and me.

The summer gets really hot, so Mom breaks down and buys a new air conditioner for her bedroom. Me and the kids drag in our mattresses and pile them all over the floor while she lies on her queen bed, looking like an invalid and scowling at us. "Pft! It's like sleepaway camp in here."

"Only it isn't any fun." Mimi flops down on her pillow.

But man, the cold air is delish, and I stand right in front of the vents, flapping up my tank top.

Mom turns on her laptop and puts on her reading glasses. "Angel, come look at these men. One jackass after another."

"Oooh, let me see a jackass," Mimi says, and she and Mossy pile around us on the bed as we check out the dating site.

"Maybe you like him?" Mimi says, pointing to a picture of a friendly-looking guy with a big, round head.

"I never met a mustache I liked," Mom says.

"Yeah, mustaches will never make a splashy comeback like bell-bottoms," I say. "Don't ever grow one," I tell Mossy.

"Why would I?" he says.

"I'm just saying, little man," I say.

"I like him," Mimi says, stabbing the screen. He's a decent-looking guy with a full head of hair, which Mom likes. His caption reads *R U Out There???* Mom clicks on his profile, which says *Looking for Beatiful sole inside and out knows how to be pleased.*

"Can't spell or write a sentence, and I ain't no fillet," Mom says.

"Why does he have to write a sentence?" Mimi says.

"Because if he can't, then he's a dummy. You want me to date a dummy?"

"This one?" Mossy points to a guy with a helmet hairdo. His caption is *Seeking Special Lady.*

Mom and I break up laughing. "See here, Mossy," she says, taking off her glasses and slinging an arm around him. "A man who calls a woman a *lady* is a bona fide jackass."

"Jackass," he whispers with glee.

"Here's a good one," I say. The guy is pretty good-looking even if he is going gray, and he looks nice, like someone you could ask for directions if you were driving around lost.

"Yeah, I saw him. He's so-so."

"I don't know, Ma. He seems better than so-so."

"Trust me. So-so."

"Fussy."

"Listen to you! You dump Joey again?"

"Why'd you dump Joey?" Mossy asks.

"I, for one, would not dump Joey," Mimi says, digging

49

her head into the crook of my arm and looking at me upside down.

"We're taking a little break," I say.

Mom smiles. "That explains Carmella." But I let that go.

Then Mossy gets a funny look. He stands on the bed and puts his finger under his nose like it's a mustache and swishes his behind. "I'm looking for a special lay-deee," he says in a high voice. We all break up.

"Do it again!" Mimi shouts.

So for the next few minutes Mossy smarms around the room with his finger mustache, coming up to each of us, saying, "Are you my special lady?" And we fall out.

"I'm a jackass!" he cries.

We laugh for a while, and it's fun to see Mom smiling, her face lit up; she looks young and pretty when she's all relaxed. When the kids finally settle down to sleep, she tiptoes into her closet and wriggles out of her nightgown and into her bra. "Angel, you up?"

"Uh-huh."

"I'm going out for a bit."

"Yeah, okay." She's on the prowl, off to hook up with one of her exes, no doubt, though I don't think that includes old TB. "Hey, Ma, where'd you see Joey and Carmella?"

"Outside 7-Eleven," she says, pulling on shorts. "So I said to him, 'I made meatballs last weekend. Where were

50

you? No Joey at my table?' Then Carmella came out with a Slurpee, and there's this dead silence." She balls up her nightgown and throws it at me. "Thanks for telling me."

"We're all friends." Of course I'm not liking the sound of this, but I'm not going to jump to conclusions either. A Slurpee. Big whoop.

"Well, I hope you're enjoying your little break." She takes her makeup bag off the nightstand, tiptoes past the sleeping kids, and disappears into the dark hallway.

"Is it me," Inggy says, "or do subs and BO smell kind of the same?"

"That's so true now that you mention it." But that doesn't stop us. The coffee table is covered with two mammoth five-foot-long subs. I rip into one with a steak knife, cutting us each a chunk. Cork's parents have gone to a wedding in North Jersey, so we're having a keg and sub party at his place.

We head into the kitchen and get tall, foamy cups of beer. Inggy grabs a can of Easy Cheese from the fridge and squirts a gob in her mouth, then in mine. I'm not one to hold a grudge, so when Joey passes by the doorway I say, "Hey, cheese man. Look what it's come to." I grab the can from Inggy and wave it at him. "Can you forgive me?" He smiles at me, a real smile, and it gives me a good feeling, like maybe a thaw is happening. I scrounge up a box of crackers from the cupboard, and Ing and I head into the yard and sit on sawhorses under a mimosa tree.

Kipper Coleman joins us, saying, "I've been thinking. . . ." Inggy squirts him a cracker, which he pops in his mouth and chews rapid-fire. "How can it be that I'll graduate high school without ever having laid my lips on either of you fine girls?" He stands there, tilting his head in a flirty way. Kipper, I should mention, is super-skinny and wears weird jeans, but he's not uncute.

"Is that my cue to jump off the sawhorse and plant one on you?" Inggy says.

"Yes, it is," he says.

"Kipper Coleman, someday you'll get laid. If you're lucky," Sherry says, waddling past with a bag of potato chips. She's four months pregnant, just starting to show, and is in a real mood these days. Honestly, she's always in a mood, but she's all right.

"Vulgar," Kipper whispers. "Here I am talking about romance and that whale completely taints the moment." The poor guy turns bright pink, only confirming that he hasn't yet done the deed.

"Aw, come here," I say. He leans in, and I plant a kiss on his hot cheek.

"Aw, my mom does that," he says.

I shrug, so he looks at Inggy, who gives him a peck on his other pink cheek, which gets him complaining again, so we hand him our cups and send him in for refills, and off he trots on his long legs.

When he comes back he says, "S'okay, if you met me in college would you think me witty and charming, or would I still be skinny old Kipper?"

"Skinny," Inggy says, "but dashing."

"You've definitely got some dash." Ing and I smile.

Then he and Ing launch into a conversation about college courses, dorms, and cafeteria plans that goes on and on.

I wander into the kitchen, and Cork strolls in with a dripping sub and holds it to my lips. I take a big old bite full of salami and onions and sweet and hot peppers, and he watches me chew. "Yummy," he says, before heading into the yard.

I'm kind of glad Carmella isn't here, but it's still early, so she'll probably show. And that's all right, I guess. A girl at the sink lights up a cigarette, and the delicious curl of smoke rising above her head makes me want one bad. I almost bum one, which kind of shocks me, but I exercise willpower and promise myself, once again, that when I'm eighty I can light up and smoke like a fiend.

I chew on a pretzel instead and have a seat next to Tank-Top Tony and play a couple of rounds of quarters with him. Tony is Sherry's off-again, on-again, the one who knocked her up. He wanted her to Hoover it once she found out, which was late, since her period's screwy to begin with and she's kind of fat. Not a tub, but definitely a muffin top. Anyhow, she was too late, so she's having a kid. Crazy.

Sherry slides into a chair.

"If you're stayin' you're playin'," Tony tells her. "And since you're obviously not drinkin', get off. Seats are for players."

"Real nice, Tony," I say.

"Bite me." Sherry slaps his arm. "If I want to watch, I'll watch!"

He sighs.

Tony and I flip quarters while Sherry scowls, and I hope Joey will come over but he doesn't. The setting sun casts a nice shadowy calm over the yard. I love this time of the day, when the afternoon seems to yawn and stretch out. It's a nice time to think, take a deep breath, consider your evening options. In the glow, Inggy and Cork sit on sawhorses, her head resting on his shoulder, his arm slung around her. What a pretty picture. She shakes the Easy Cheese and he opens his mouth and she squirts him a glob. Then she makes herself a cracker.

I keep right on drinking, and at some point it dawns on me that I am one tipsy girl. When Joey passes the kitchen doorway and heads upstairs, I follow him. When he opens the bathroom door, I'm right behind him.

"What the hell, Angel?"

"Sit a minute." I close the toilet lid, have a seat, and wait for him to sit on the rim of the tub. Instead he opens the medicine cabinet, roots around, finds some dental floss, and starts sawing it between his teeth. I watch in the mirror.

"How long, Joe?" I ask. But he just keeps on flossing. Finally he tosses the string and has a look at his teeth. "Joey?"

"Can I pee?"

"Come on. I asked you a question."

"Will you get out, please?"

Please? There's something so awful about that *please*. Like we're strangers, instead of us. Me and Joey. Who've been naked together many times.

"Just stop. I'm done, Angel. Okay? I'm done."

But I can't move.

He yanks me off the bowl, opens the door, and leans in close. "You toy with me. Honest to God, you do. Maybe you don't even know it. It's over, okay?" I back out of the bathroom and he shuts the door quick, almost hitting me.

chapter 6

I sleep late, and when I take a look around the room, I see that the kids are gone and their covers are balled up on their mattresses. Even Mom is up and out. The shades are down and cold air blasts from the AC. I dive back under the sheet to sleep some more.

"Are you sick, Angel?" Mimi says a while later, kneeling beside me.

"Yeah, a little," I say, pushing hair out of my eyes.

"I'll be the nurse. What do you need?" She's wearing glitter eye shadow, a bikini, and feather boa.

"How about a Coke, Meems." I squint at the clock. It's nearly eleven-thirty, which is when I'm supposed to be at work. "Where's Ma?"

Mimi makes her fingers like scissors. "Haircut," she says. "Are you contagious?"

I shake my head.

"You're sad, aren't you?"

"A little."

She runs off and comes back with a glass of Coke loaded with cubes, and Mossy troops in behind her. "Hand me the phone, will you, my little man?" I say.

I dial the marina while they kneel on the floor, watching. Finally I get Dad. "I'm not feeling too hot," I tell him as I walk into the hallway, where the heat is stifling. "I'll come in, though, if you're stuck."

"No, honey, don't worry. Are you all right?"

"Yeah, I don't know. It's my head. . . . I don't know. I'll be fine." I take the phone into the bathroom and look at my frizzy, sleepy, hungover self in the mirror.

"Take some Advil and take it easy. We'll work it out here."

"Hey, Dad, thanks," I say, sitting on the toilet lid.

"You're my girl," he says, which always kind of gets me.

"It's just that Joey—"

"Hold on a sec, hon. . . . Yeah. Check the invoice. No, the other pile. . . . Hey, Angel, we'll have dinner soon, okay?"

"All right." And I hold the phone to my ear until I realize he's hung up. I pad back into the bedroom and fall on the deliciously cold mattress and close my eyes.

The kids come back in with a bag of bread, jars of peanut butter and jelly, and a butter knife. I don't think I want a sandwich, but when Mimi slaps one together and holds it to my lips, I take a nibble and realize I'm starved and could eat my arm. Plus it's really good. I sit up and join the picnic, the kids yakking and breathing peanut butter and jelly breath on me. Meems asks if I'm still feeling funky and I say it's probably a long-lasting funk. Mossy wants to know how long, so I say a week at least. Is it Joey? they want to know. I confess that yeah, it is.

"You keep dumping him!" Mimi says.

"Not this time."

She cocks her head. "He dumped *you*? I'll smack his face!"

Mossy scratches a mosquito bite. "He blew up my raft," he says.

"And he found the leak," I remind him. Mossy nods.

"And now," Mimi cries, "he won't blow up anything else ever again!"

"Maybe not." I flop back on the pillow and close my eyes. *I'm done, Angel. I'm done.*

"I'll smack his face," Mimi says.

And we lounge around feeling lousy for a few minutes before Mossy pats my head with a sticky hand and says, "Let's go to the beach." Might as well, so I head outside in my nightshirt and sunglasses and pluck my bikini off the line.

It's another scorcher, without a cloud in the sky. The kids hop all around me, holding my hands, as we head up the street. We climb the stairs and walk over the bridge to the sand, where I flash the badge checker my season pass. Funny how as soon as the kids glimpse the water they charge toward it, as if they've never seen the ocean before. They race down to the shoreline, dropping their towels along the way, and fling themselves into the waves. How great it is to be a kid. Watching them makes me feel a little bit old. And that's how I spend my first totally-Joey-free, no-more-hope-for-Joey day.

Summer moves on, and so do I. August comes and there's plenty going on—pumping gas, hanging out with Inggy, going to the beach, parties. We even meet at school one day for cheerleading practice and dance around the dried-up brown grass to "Pocketful of Sunshine," doing some half-assed handsprings before collapsing on the grass and smoking a joint.

Carmella flops down next to me. "We okay, Angel?" she whispers. She and Joey are official. I nod. Inggy passes her the joint and she takes a long drag and holds her breath before exhaling toward the sky. Then she turns to me and smiles.

"It's all right," I tell her. Actually, I think I'll get him back. Not now, but maybe when school rolls around. It's okay. Mostly.

I go for a boat ride with madras guy and that leads to another, then another, until his girlfriend gets wind of it. The girlfriend is news to me, but that's a guy for you.

Vic and I hang out more too. First as friends, playing rummy on top of the slide, waiting to plunk the occasional kid on a burlap sack and give him a shove down. Vic likes to man the slide better than the Ferris wheel because it's less work, meaning from nine to midnight there's only the lone kid or two climbing the stairs with a sack, which means we can hang out, drink hard lemonade, and listen to the waves slap the shore. Plus the view. Oh, I love the view!

Usually working a ride on the boardwalk is a complete loser job unless you're fourteen and too young to get anything else, but Vic's uncle is part owner of the amusement park and a Polish mobster, to boot. He wears a Guido tank and a diamond ring. A complete cliché, but I have to say he's a pretty nice guy. He pays Vic a ridiculously good wage in cash, opening his fat wallet and wetting a finger before flipping through a major wad of fifties and twenties. When I'm there he'll peel off a few more twenties and give Vic a playful slap across the head and say, "Buy your pretty girlfriend here somethin' nicer than a sausage sandwich, huh?"

So Vic and I have a midsummer adventure. How good and horny it feels, zooming around the island on his Vespa, weaving in and out of benny traffic, the wind in our hair, my arms tight around his abs, him leaning back and kissing me at red lights. *And here it begins*. We even have surf and turf one night, courtesy of the mobster.

Meanwhile our renters come and go—the benny families flapping around in their flip-flops and 45 sunblock. Mom flirts with the better-looking husbands. Late one night when I'm walking my bike over the stones to the shed, I catch a glimpse of a couple entwined by the rosebush. My flustered mom comes tripping around the corner when she hears me, saying, "I was just showing Ned our roses."

"Uh-huh," I say, strolling past. The guy smiles too big and sticks his nose right into one of the flowers. It's some pretty sorry acting.

Minutes later, when I'm eating a Ring Ding at the kitchen counter, Mom comes traipsing in with a little smile on her face. "That wasn't what it looked like."

"Ma, you were totally making out with the dude."

She cocks her head and shrugs.

Her personal ad brings a slew of responses but not a single date. They're too old, too fat, aging badly, or mustached. There's a black guy who likes "cream in his coffee" and a guy who would "seriously like to kick ass like Arnold Schwarzenegger." So she makes do with the exes, waiting until the next Mr. Right comes along. Sometimes she leaves for the night and returns in the morning, and when Tofu Bart starts looking happier and gets a spring in his step, I think even he's getting lucky.

And then there's a heat wave like none other. Some days it's so hot the air looks wavy. The kids have sweaty pink faces like someone blew them up, leaving them hot and moist. I pump gas in my bikini and baseball cap and spritz myself with the hose every five seconds. My dad sets up a big beach umbrella on the dock that I sit under, but even with a portable fan plugged into the generator I think I'm going to spontaneously combust.

Speaking of Dad, we mean to have dinner, but it never exactly works out. We do have lunch some days in his crammed office, sharing a meatball or chicken parm sub while Joop lies at our feet and the blasting air conditioner whirls invoices into the air.

Deep into August the heat still hasn't broken. It's steamy for days, and everyone walks around glistening with sweat, looking dazed. And there's a west wind, which means the beach is no relief because it brings biting green flies. You can catch a breeze up there, but you'll be slapping your arms and legs the whole time.

Inggy's sprawled out on the dock and Cork's standing over her. "Do I have to carry you?" But she's either asleep or ignoring him. She just came back from another college visit and then worked a double at Sundae Times. Cork has his brother's 32 Carolina Classic tonight and is taking us to the flats to cool off.

"So tired . . . ," she mumbles. She has a glob of hot fudge in her hair.

"Will you stop?" Cork hoists her up, and she dangles like a rag doll and lets out a tired laugh.

"Seriously, no. I'm so beat."

"The ride will wake you."

"Home, Cork. I'm going home."

"Come on, Ing," I say. "It'll be fun."

He bends and heaves her onto his shoulder, and her long white hair touches the dock.

"Knock it off," she says upside down. He carries her down the length of the dock to have a fight with her, I guess, and we can hear them both complaining.

"Looks like we're not going anywhere," Sherry says, holding her round stomach.

"Ye of little faith," I say. "We're going."

"And freaking Tony doesn't show up. He said he was coming."

Everyone was supposed to come—Joey too—but here it is just Sherry and me. Soon Ing calls out, "Bye, you guys."

"Don't bail," I yell, but she's already on her bike.

Cork lopes back, making a face. "Ready?" He swings himself onto the gunnel.

"I have to pee like every half hour, so I hope that bathroom's clean," Sherry says.

"Sorry," he says. "Doesn't work."

"Forget it, then," she says. "I'm not going."

"Pee in the water," he tells her.

Sherry puts her hands on her hips and stares at us unhappily before flapping away in her flip-flops.

"Oh, come on," I call. But she waves a hand over her head and keeps walking.

"Crap, everybody's bailing. So it's just you and me?" I ask.

"Looks like."

I swing myself over the side. "You still want to go?"

"Yeah, don't you?"

"I'm game. Definitely." And we're off. It's good to speed around in the boat, the wind rushing over us. Oh, how guys love to speed. So we ride around for a while, our hair flying out behind us, and then we head to the flats, anchoring in the deeper part.

I have to pee and reach for the bathroom door. "Shoot," I say, remembering.

Cork steps in front of me and opens the door. "It works."

"Oh, you did not!"

He climbs down the ladder into the water and floats out on his back, making ripples. "Sherry's wound pretty tight. Am I right or am I wrong?"

"She's knocked up, Cork."

"Knocked up, hopped up. She would have bitched the whole time."

"Have a heart."

"All hopped up, I'm telling you. All you girls are hopped up." He splashes water at me.

"You're an ass."

"Okay, I'm an ass," he says, paddling up to the ladder. "Okay, Ing's mostly not hopped up." He closes one eye, thinking. "And you, Cassonetti, I have to say, you are not hopped up."

"I know."

"Are you coming in or are you standing there?"

I slip into the warm water and a strand of seaweed twirls around my wrist like a bracelet. I swim over to a sandbar where the water's only a few inches deep and lie there on the sandy bottom. How weird and wild to be in the middle of the bay in a few inches of water. It's a moonless night and the sky is inky. With my head tipped back I feel like I'm floating in space, surrounded by black water and night. A whiff of fish fills the air.

Cork swims over and we both drink in the dark sky until it starts to rain lightly. We huddle down in the warm water while the cold drops hit our faces; one runs into my ear, making me yelp. It's just a quick, delicious shower, and when it's over Cork starts to entertain me. He walks in the shallow water going "do da do." Like a clueless clown, he walks with exaggerated steps, then drops off in deep water, letting himself sink with gurgles and bubbles. After a few tries, he gets the timing perfect, and it's pretty funny.

He swims to the boat and comes back with a raft. I lie

on it, and he pulls me into the deeper water, then hangs onto the side as we rock with the tide. We float along, not talking, and it's nice.

"Had enough?" Cork says, paddling us toward the shallow water.

"I don't know. It's so much cooler here."

"Yeah," he says, lifting his wet head.

"Hey," I say, "you think Joey will come around?"

"Why you asking me?"

"You're his friend."

"So are you."

"Not anymore, I don't think."

"You're so different, you guys." He blinks his watery lashes at me.

"Different's okay." A tiny crab, ghostly pale, smaller than my thumb, scuttles past. I finger the top of its shell and it spins around, lost and teensy, all of its legs flailing.

We float up onto the sandbar in a few inches of water. Cork stretches out along the bottom and rests his head on the raft. I flip on my stomach and yawn, breathing in wet rubber.

"You have a sweet ass, Cassonetti."

"Hey, thanks."

"I'd like to spank that juicy behind."

I flick him on the forehead with two fingers.

"Ouch," he says, and laughs.

I close my eyes, feeling lulled by the current and growing sleepy.

Just as my eyes grow heavy, Cork puts his hand inside my bikini bottom and rubs my ass. Real slow. Everything stops for a moment. For a long minute nothing happens except for Cork rubbing my naked ass. In slow motion, I turn my head to look at him, and it's clear that if he looks at me the spell might break, so he doesn't.

"John Cork," I whisper, making him meet my eyes, which he does, looking all dreamy and not quite inside himself. For a long minute we stare at each other, and it feels like something's getting decided.

He kisses me, hungry and soft. My favorite way.

Once, twice, again and again. "Sit up," he says. I slip off the raft and kneel in the water next to him. He cups my face and we kiss until our legs grow numb.

"Here." He sits in the shallow water, pulls me onto his lap, and presses me to him, all warm and wet and smelling and tasting like gasoline, sweat, and black salty water. He buries his face between my boobs and I feel him smile. It's the quiet, maybe—the lapping water, the lone flapping of wings in the sky—that makes it all seem unreal. The raft drifts away. Cork follows my eyes and says, "Let it."

He slowly unties my bikini strings and lets the top drop. And he does something very sexy. He doesn't look but stares into my eyes for an endless minute, a smile on his lips. Only then does he let his eyes drop. And when he does I shiver. "Oh, you," he says. "Fantastic boobage."

And here it begins comes uninvited into my brain. *No, no,* I tell myself, burying my face in his neck. *Not this. This is nothing.*

We really go at it then. Naked in the middle of the bay, we do it with me sitting on his lap.

It's late when we climb back into the boat.

"It won't count," I whisper.

"I want it to count," he says, reaching for the keys.

I shake my head. "Don't be stupid." But I wrap myself around him, and he lifts me into a piggyback and starts the motor.

We putter away, cutting a rough path through the water. I think about Inggy asleep in her bed with the dust ruffle, curled up on her side, wrapped in her white hair, dreaming, maybe. Safe there. She's been safe all her life.

Up ahead we see the raft drifting on the smooth surface. Cork cuts the engine, and using a net, he captures it and fishes it out. "There," he says, satisfied.

fall

chapter 7

I'm back in the Corner House.

It's a cool September night with a wind kicking around. He whistles low at the back door, standing there in his GUARD sweatshirt, hood up, eyeing me. I come to the screen and lean into it. "So what do you want?"

"A blow job."

I laugh. "You're an ass."

I unlatch the door, walk into the kitchen, and eat another meatball from the bubbling pot, a midnight snack. Cork comes up behind me and wraps around me. I feel him. "Have a meatball, McHardon." I stab one, hold it out. He bites, chews, and kisses me with saucy lips.

"Sooo good."

"I know." I turn off the stove and he follows me up the stairs, his finger twisted around my belt loop. Halfway up he unzips my jeans and puts his finger inside me. We fall, bumping down a couple of steps.

"You're wet," he says, his hot breath in my ear.

At the top of the steps he picks me up. I wrap my legs around him, and he walks into the bedroom and drops us on the bed. We tumble and roll, his lips on my neck, trailing down my throat. I yank off his jeans and underwear, he yanks off mine. And soon he's inside me, pumping hard. I like it hard. I like it fast. Both of us free-falling.

I thought it would be weird at school. Our lockers are right across from each other, and the three of us always hang out before homeroom. But it's okay. We're the same. We can look each other right in the eyes, me and Cork. We don't give anything away. Me and Cork. Me and Inggy. Me, Inggy, and Cork. All of us friends. The same as always. Sometimes, though, he'll come up to me between classes and whisper in my ear, "Later, Cassonetti."

Night is when it happens. Him standing at my back door, the cool darkness of summer becoming fall, the wind through the screen, the crickets chirping, him looking in, waiting for me. I love the first glimpse of him standing there where he doesn't belong—in the yellowed porch light next to the mimosa tree. His dick hard, his heart beating. I'm slow to open the door. It's always late, the day softly fuzzed into night. We never say much, me and Cork. I like Cork in the dark, the feel of his heat and his mouth hot and wet on mine. I'm not exactly me, and he's not exactly him. But here we are.

I can stop it anytime. And I will. It's not cool. It just isn't. But this is my first fall, and doesn't everyone fall sooner or later? I'm basically good. Yeah, I copy homework sometimes and sometimes cheat on tests—who doesn't. But I don't lie. Not really, not about the stuff that counts. So I'm allowed this little thing. Plus I don't love Cork. He loves Inggy and she loves him. They're meat and potatoes. I'm just a dessert. I won't let it go on too long. And Inggy can never, ever know. Cork will never tell. I'll never tell. She won't know.

Inggy. I wonder if someday when we're like eighty—when I allow myself to smoke like a fiend—I wonder if one day when we're, say, sitting on folding chairs under an umbrella on the beach, me sucking on my smoke and Inggy upwind of it, I wonder if I could say, *Cork and I had a thing—a little fling back in senior year. Did you know?*

Get out, she'd say. We'll both be grandmothers, maybe great-grandmothers. It's possible. Inggy won't have married Cork. I don't see that in her stars, though it's hard to tell what she sees. She doesn't know what college will do for her. I mean, of course she knows what it will do for her. But she doesn't know how it will change the basic fact of her and Cork. He'll go to Ocean Community with me, if anything, and Inggy will meet new guys, smart guys, and slowly Cork will be uncorked. I know it. I bet he knows it. Only she doesn't.

But I'm rambling. Back to the future: we'll have married, we'll have maybe a couple divorces between us. I hope not, but it happens. And I'll say, *Did you know? About me and Cork?* She won't have, but if she chews it over for a few days she'll say, *Yeah, I'm not completely shocked.* And she'll have a secret or two herself, it'll turn out. It won't be my kind of secret, but she'll have something good, and we'll laugh into each other's wrinkled faces—my wrinkles will be worse since Ing slathers up with 45 sunblock.

It'll be okay. I'll say sorry, and she'll shrug a little sorrowfully. And I'll say that in the end friendship is the most lasting thing. Maybe we'll have outlived our husbands. It's possible. And she'll agree. We'll be sexed out by then, so it won't be a big deal.

Maybe, though, it's better if Inggy never knows. Not even if we're old and grandmothers and all sexed out. Some things you just keep to yourself always.

Afterwards we lie twisted in my sheet and sweaty. A cool wind blows off the bay. We lie close and breathe.

Cork is skinny. In his clothes, he's bigger somehow. Naked next to me, he's lean and hard, with pale hair on his long arms and legs. His belly button is botched, a round button that would look right on a fat man. I like that it's all wrong. His dick is small and soft, and his breathing slows. I give him a nudge.

"You booting me already?" he says with closed eyes.

"Don't fall asleep."

"Five minutes."

"Yeah, okay," I say.

He does his putting-on-his-pants dance—little hops around the room as he hoists them up. Then he sits on the edge of the bed.

"See you tomorrow." I touch my fingers to his back.

"Yup." He slides his feet into his flip-flops. "Has she said anything?"

"Like what?" I ask.

"She doesn't know, right?"

"She doesn't know. You worried?"

"Nah."

I sit up and give him a hug, pressing my boobs into his back. "Have a meatball on the way out."

"She'd hate me," he says.

"I'm pretty sure we'd both be in deep shit."

"Yeah, but she'd hate me," he says matter-of-factly.

I look at him. "You're an ass."

He pins me in one quick move and climbs on top of me. "Stop calling me an ass."

"Stop being one."

And this gets us hot. When I break free, I unzip him and tug at his shirt.

Later, when he goes, I hear the squeak of the screen and his crunch over the stones. I feel full and curl up in the middle of the bed.

chapter 8

After school one day we're sitting at my kitchen table eating cookies. Mossy's sweaty and pink from pushing a puck around the street with his hockey stick. "So, Mossy," Inggy says, slinging an arm around him and with her other hand pinching a Thin Mint from the wrapper. "Where would you take a girl on a date?"

"I don't like girls," he says, sharpening a pencil.

"You like us," I say.

He checks the point and goes back to twisting the pencil. "You and Inggy. Mom. Mrs. Fishbaum and Mimi sometimes."

"Okay, let's say you're taking *me* on date," Ing says. "Where do you take me?"

"Dairy Queen."

"Good choice." Ing and I smile across the table. "Do you pay?"

"How much?" he asks, a little exasperated.

"Well," Ing says. "Let's say we have burgers, fries, and two thick shakes. So let's say fifteen bucks."

He shakes his head. "Nope."

I lean across the table and whisper in his ear. "That's not very romantic, my little man."

"Okay, the playground," he says. "Girls like swings."

"While Inggy's on the swings what will you do?"

"Ride my board on the dock."

"But then it's not a date," I say. "You have to do it together, see."

He dunks a cookie in his milk and pops the whole thing in his mouth and chews slowly. "I'm not going on the swings," he says finally. "You want a ride on the back of my scooter?"

"That sounds romantic," she says. "I'll have the wind in my hair. Then afterwards will you buy me a Dilly Bar?"

He looks up at her pretty face and blushes. "Okay," he says.

"I'm going to have to marry you," Inggy tells him.

"I'm eight," he tells her in that totally serious kid way.

"I'm forced to wait."

He tests out the point of his pencil. "Let's think of all the words we can for *butt*."

"Let's," Ing says. "*Tush, ass, derriere.*"

"*Booty* and *patootie* and *behind*," I add.

Mossy scribbles away. "Don't forget *can*," he says. "And *bum*. That's what they say in England. *Bum*."

"You're very worldly, my man," I tell him.

"Maid service," Mom says, coming in with a clean load of laundry. She dumps towels, sheets, and underwear in a pile on the couch. "You do the next load," she tells me.

"Yup."

"You have great undies, Angel," Inggy says, eyeing the heap. "I like that silver pair."

"Oh, that's mine." Mom plucks the thong from the pile and gives it a twirl before stuffing it half in her jeans pocket.

"Oh, a thong." Inggy leans over and covers Mossy's ears. "I hate the string up my crack."

"You get used to it," Mom says.

"I don't know," I say, "either it works for you or it doesn't." I personally love thongs and have always been surprised about Ing's thong issue, but there you go. I'm sure Cork's given her a hard time, because like any horndog he loves them. *Come on, Ing,* he'd say. *For me. Nope,* she'd say. *I want to see the little triangle riding up your tailbone when you bend over in your jeans. Sorry,* she'd say.

Sometimes, just sometimes, I find myself wondering about them really going at it. I know that sounds kind of pervy, me wondering about my friends in bed. And it's not like I want a ringside seat or anything. I sure don't. But here's what's kind of weird and interesting when you think about it. That that part of you—the naked, horny you—is tucked away, hidden. I mean, the only people who know what you're like in the sack are the people you've been

79

with. It's this whole other life and with each guy a new secret. I love that.

"Earth to Angel," Mom says.

"What?"

"You didn't tell me all the places Inggy's applying."

"I can't keep track of them all."

"Good luck, honey," Mom tells her.

"Thanks." Inggy ducks her head shyly. "Cornell might be my first choice, but I don't know."

"Inggy has *choices*," I say, slinging an arm around her. We smirk at each other.

"If you cracked open a book now and then you'd have choices too," she says.

Mom sighs. "I was the same way. . . . Hey, how about real estate, Angel?"

"Real estate!"

"You take some courses, get a license, sell houses."

"Who said I want to sell houses!"

"So don't sell houses." Mom shrugs. "I'm just saying."

"You'll figure it out," Inggy says, but she doesn't look so sure. Which sorta pisses me off. I'm seventeen. Do I need to decide my life this second?

"Ma, what's another word for *butt*?" Mossy asks.

"*Fanny*. As in get your fanny in the House and find Oscar. He escaped."

"No, he didn't. He's right here." Mossy reaches into his

80

sweatshirt pocket and holds up the little mouse with his twitching nose and whiskers.

Inggy shrieks.

"Mossy and Oscar are a package deal," I tell her.

"Then I will find a place in my heart for Oscar."

"He's very small for a mouse." Mossy cups him in his palm.

"Hello there, Oscar," Mom says. "I had you pegged for an escape artist."

"He does look a little sneaky," Inggy says, running a finger down Oscar's quivering back.

"Knock, knock," a voice says.

"Look who it is. Hello, handsome," Mom says.

"Hey, Mrs. Rossi," Joey says.

I go to the screen and he motions me outside. I hear Inggy whisper, "Maybe somebody's getting interested."

"No practice?" I ask, joining him in the yard.

He shakes his head. "Early one this morning." He hasn't shaved and his hair is long and flipping up on the ends, and he's wearing an unzipped sweatshirt and a T-shirt that says EAT BACON above a sizzling strip.

"Thought I'd say hi," he says, lowering his eyes and then looking back at me. His eyes are dark and soft. Oh, how I like Joey Sardone.

"It's about time."

"So what are you up to?"

"The usual." I smooth out the stones with my flip-flop. "Nothing so interesting."

"Yeah, right." He smiles. "In third period I look up from my Spanish quiz and there you are walking along the ledge."

"Oh, that."

So I tell him. I was sitting on the radiator in humanities and leaning out the window and fiddling with my bracelet when I accidentally dropped it on the outside ledge. My dad gave it to me when I was little and I eventually grew into it. It's silver and threaded with small sapphires. Very delicate, pretty, not exactly my taste, but it was a gift from him. So I got a pass to the girls' room, climbed out on the second-story ledge, and walked past the Spanish classes to humanities, where I rescued my bracelet. Pickett, my teacher, who must be eighty, opened the window wide and when I tried to tell her I was fine she reached for me with her age-spotted hands and hauled me in, then sent me straight to the office, where I stayed all afternoon. You really have to think about the logic of that, me missing all my afternoon classes.

"I swung by the office after school," Joey says, "but it didn't look like you had detention."

"Nah, Costello"—that's our principal—"was having a root canal, and it was just the office ladies. Myrtle had to visit her mom at the nursing home and Tammy was headed for the super saver at Grand Union. To buy creamed corn. I kid you not. Creamed corn, whatever that is."

"Sounds like something in a can."

"Totally."

"So you're off the hook?"

"Yeah. Costello just said, 'Really, Angel,' and gave me the evil eye. I pointed out that the ledge is like two or three feet wide at least and I could practically do a cartwheel on it, to which Myrtle said I need to have my head examined." I shrug.

"Troublemaker." He taps my flip-flop with his sneaker and smiles. "Kinda makes me miss you."

"I kinda miss you."

Mom comes out with the empty laundry basket, the thong pushing out of her pocket. "How's every little thing, Joey Sardone?"

"Pretty darn good," he says, happily enough.

"Glad to hear it." We all smile.

We watch her walk into the House, the laundry basket bouncing off her hip. "She misses you too. Obviously," I say. "You like Carmella?"

"Yeah, I like Carmella," he snaps.

"Okay, you like Carmella."

"I should go." He touches my shoulder and walks.

"It's weird not to hang out with you," I say, following behind and crunching over the stones. "Seeing you all the time at school . . ."

"We say hey."

I shove him.

"I have a girlfriend," he says, turning back and zipping his sweatshirt.

"So? You have a girlfriend. Fine."

"You don't follow any of the rules, do you?"

I lean against the side of the house and wonder for a sec if he knows. But no, he doesn't know about me and Cork. "Gluteus maximus," I barely hear Inggy say, and Mossy goes, "I think I've heard of that."

"Do you ever think the rules are bullshit?" I ask.

Joey leans next to me against the house. I think he's going to kiss me, and my heart starts to make a little racket, but he doesn't, of course.

"I loved you, Angel."

"Really?" I look up at his shy face, bright under the cool eaves of the house.

"Uh-huh."

"How did you know?" I ask.

"What do you mean how did I know?"

I touch him. "I mean, what did you love about me?"

"I can't dissect it."

"But what did it feel like?"

"What a question." He pulls away. "I just knew. All right?"

I wonder about Carmella, if he loves her, and if it happens to him all the time. Maybe it does for some people. But it must be special, love.

"I do miss you, you know." He pulls a half-eaten Twix from his pocket and takes a bite and holds out what's left.

"You eat it," I say.

He eats the last bite, crumples the wrapper, and sticks it in his pocket. I reach in and take it out. "I'll toss it for you."

"Well, I should go," he says, turning. I jump on his back for old times' sake. He makes a soft groan but hoists up my legs and carries me alongside the house to the front stoop, where he drops me. I watch him walk along the bay, his hands buried in his pockets.

Inggy's on the phone with Cork, I can tell. She looks into the middle distance when she talks to him, half bored, half dreamy. I slide into the seat next to Mossy and take his hand. "I'm back."

"Hi." He glances up to me. "Look," he says, showing me the list. Then he says, "Ew, you're hot." It's true, his small hand feels so cool in mine.

"Don't you think Angel and Joey should give it another go?" Inggy says into the phone. "She is not. Oh, stop."

I scan Mossy's list. "You forgot *rear end*."

"Of course!" he yells. He scribbles like mad and grabs the list and runs out the back door.

"Bye," Inggy yells. "Save our wedding date." Then she says, "Gotta go," into the phone.

I take the crumpled candy wrapper out of my pocket and smooth it flat. Joey loved me. "What did Cork say I am?"

She laughs and flips her hand.

"What'd he say?"

"He was talking crap."

My phone blips in my back pocket.

"Ing, around what age do you think you can consider yourself sophisticated?"

"Probably twenty-six," she says. "Well, I should go study for calc. We're having potato pancakes. Want to come over?" she says, gathering up her stuff.

"We're having chicken parm."

"Well now," she says, tilting her blond head. "Maybe I'm staying."

"Totally stay."

But she slides out of the chair. "Carmella won't last, you know."

"But I wouldn't either. I'd keep ending it. Joey's good, isn't he?"

She swings her bag onto her shoulder and lets out a sigh. "It's noble of you not to diddle him around."

I get up and bring the glasses to the sink. "Oh, I'm not so noble."

"You sorta are."

I toss the wrapper, turn on the water, and squirt the sponge with lemony detergent. "What did Cork call me? You said 'She is not.'"

"It was nothing, I told you," she says. When I glance over, she's digging in her bag and I can't tell if it was nothing or if she doesn't want to say. Out the window a seagull eats something stringy from the ground. Ing tugs my hair before heading out. "See ya."

I reach for my phone with a wet hand. Cork's text says "Later."

chapter 9

At halftime me and Ing and some of the girls smoke a joint and get the giggles. When the band plays our rally song we spin on the sidelines with our shakers high in the air, and the music swells in my bones and Inggy's bones and everyone's bones, as if we're all connected. Inggy swoops down and hugs me. "My friend," she says. "No, my friend," I say.

Now, in the fourth quarter, we're down by ten, and a light rain is falling. We quit the cheers and some of the girls huddle under umbrellas while Carmella keeps springing over to the bench where Joey sits with a bag of ice on his knee. She plops onto his lap until a coach shoos her away and then she flies back to us only to sprint back once more, as if the electrical current between them is too much to keep her away. Cork leans over the fence, watching Ing, and she prances up and plants one on him.

"Stoner," he says.

"True," she says. They kiss over the fence.

The only one with pep is Mimi, who's wearing her Pop

Warner cheerleading uniform. She climbs the fence and waits for me to lift her over. As soon as I do, she springs into action, waving her shakers and shouting to the bleachers, "We've got spirit, we've got class, come on now, let's get some sass." I do a couple of cheers with her until I run out of steam.

The drizzle stops, but the sun stays hidden. Feeling restless, I do a back handspring and muddy my hands. From where I stand I count three guys in the bleachers I slept with, another leaning on the fence. Then I count Joey and move in a half circle and count two more guys on the field and the assistant to the assistant coach, who doesn't really count 'cause I only gave him a blow job. Then I lose count. I rub on cherry lip gloss, blinking into mist.

I love the moment when the guy is mine, when the spell is cast. Everything else falls away and there's only me and him. I wonder if there's a right love and a wrong love. Is getting naked with a cute guy and watching his eyes soften and feeling my heart pound high in my chest—is that a little like the real thing?

After the game, TB's taking the kids to Olive Garden for an early dinner. I walk Mimi to his car, where Mossy my man sits all patient in the backseat, and think isn't it funny how when you're a kid so much of your life is planned for you. You just show up. There he sits, waiting for what's next.

"Get in," TB says through the window. "You need some nutrition after all that hopping around."

"Nah. I have plans. But thanks," I say.

"You love Olive Garden," Mimi says, giving me a yank. True, but Mom's got a date tonight and no doubt TB wants to grill me on the specifics.

"Bring me back a breadstick," I tell her.

I walk into the school, where Inggy's in the locker room combing her shiny though staticky hair and putting on lip gloss.

I lie down on the bench. "Want to hang out, Ing?"

"I'm going over Cork's," she says, and in a lower voice, "Pot makes me horny."

"Okay."

"We'll give you a ride."

Cork's parked in the back of the school lot, where he lies across the hood of his mom's Camry, and he lazily turns his head to us as we walk up. "What the feck, Ing? I'm waiting forever."

"Poor baby," she says, slapping his leg.

I slap his other leg for good measure and head to the backseat.

Sherry whistles and motions Inggy or me or maybe both of us over. "I'll go see her," Inggy says, and trots off.

Cork climbs in the front, and here we are, serendipitously, together. I poke him. "Come over later. After the party."

"You know, I'm not at your beck and call." He looks out the window.

"Yeah, so? You think I'm at yours?"

He turns on the engine, and the car rumbles. "Did I sound like a dick?"

"Pretty much," I say.

"You think we should stop?"

"No. But I would. I mean, if you want to."

"I would too if you want to."

"We're willing," I say, as if it means something.

Cork nods but still doesn't look at me.

"What's up?" I climb clumsily into the front seat, my skirt riding high on my thighs.

He puts on a pair of dark sunglasses and checks himself in the rearview mirror. "Sometimes I feel like a dickweed. Mostly not, you know, but sometimes."

"So today you feel like a dickweed?"

"Yeah, Cassonetti, today I feel like a dickweed."

"Look at me," I say.

He takes off the glasses and locks eyes with me. I try to read him but I see what I always see: a soft smile and his eyes at a low burn.

He slides his hand under my cheerleading skirt and hooks the crotch of my underwear. We both watch Inggy out the window. She has an arm around Sherry and they're talking with their faces down. Sherry's due in a few weeks and her belly is impossibly huge. Fall leaves swirl around their feet. What is it about swirling yellowed leaves that makes me feel sad? Cork slides his finger in and out of me—wet and slow and delicious. I let my eyes close for a second.

Inggy walks back to the car, head down in the wind. Cork pulls out his finger and sticks it in his mouth, giving it a quick suck. I climb into the backseat and smooth down my skirt. Inggy opens the front door and hops in.

Sometimes a little peace and quiet is nice, but I kind of wish somebody was around. Mom's having her nails done before her date and it's just too quiet. In the House, I eat out of the fridge—a hunk of cheddar cheese, a handful of baby carrots, some cold mashed potatoes. I call Vic on a whim but it goes right to voice mail, and then I sit at the table all by my lonesome and suck on a cherry ice pop.

In the Corner House, I run water in the tub and wash my hair and soak in the tub. Then, wrapped in towels, I take a nap. When I wake, it's fully dark and I go back over to the House and eat some Wheat Thins with cream cheese and slices of pepperoni before getting the idea of visiting my dad.

• • •

Lily and Abby press their noses against the glass and jump up and down, yelling, "Angel!" Lily's four and Abby's nearly three and they each have high pigtails shooting out the sides of their heads like little fire hydrants.

"Hello, monkeys," I say to them.

My dad ushers me into the kitchen. "Sit and eat something, honey."

"We're doing cleanup," Ginger says. "Leftovers." She's pear-shaped with frizzy hair she pulls back in a scrunchie, but she has a pretty smile when she smiles, which isn't often.

"No worries, I'm not hungry," I lie. "I've been foraging in the fridge."

Ginger opens lids and sniffs things.

"I'm having spaghetti," Abby tells me.

"And I'm having a pork chop." Lily leaps across the linoleum.

"Here's some eggplant rotini," Ginger says doubtfully. The gravy is hardened around the edges and laced with water droplets.

"Really, I ate," I say.

"Foraging isn't a meal," Dad says. "I'll make you some spaghetti with olive oil, garlic, and red pepper." One of my favorites.

"Darn, we only have enough spaghetti for Abby." Ginger presses her hand to my arm. "Sorry. Saturday is cleanup day and Sunday is food shopping."

That's my cue; I should go. I really should. "I'll take a cookie or a Coke. Or nothing. Really. I'm easy."

"We don't keep soda in the house anymore. Empty calories, you know." Ginger comes up with a half-eaten box of animal crackers and a half glass of pomegranate juice to which she adds a splash of tap water. She hands it to me with a quick smile. Then as she heats up the assorted meals in the microwave she does squats. "I'm multitasking," she tells me.

I'm saved by Lily, who doesn't want to eat sitting down. She wanders around the living room, nibbling on the greasy pork and giving karate chops to the couch and recliner. When Ginger gets a phone call, Lily and I wander off to her bedroom and sit at a little plastic table.

"I missed you, Angel," Lily says tipping her face up at me. "Would you like a lobster or fried egg?"

"A lobster would be yummy." She chucks the pork chop into the toy box, wiggles into a tutu, and serves me a plastic lobster on a plate. "Enjoy," she says. Then she trots over with the tea service. "How many lumps?" She grabs a handful of plastic sugar cubes.

"Three," I say. She daintily drops them in my cup one at time, looking pleased.

Ginger pokes her head into the room and watches us. "Where is the pork chop, young lady?"

Lily's eyes grow wide. "Angel ate it."

Ginger gives me the death glare. I'm not kidding, the death glare.

"Hey, I'm enjoying a lobster." I wave it in the air. "You might want to check the toy box."

She screws up her face and her head must momentarily shrivel too, because her scrunchie suddenly wilts to the side. She marches over to the box and flings the toys around and finally holds up the gnawed-on chop. "What is this?" she screams at Lily. "Is this what you do with your dinner?"

Dad rescues me and steers me out the room. "What a nuthouse, huh? Come have my ravioli. I insist," he whispers.

"I'm good," I say, beelining for the door and grabbing my jacket and bag. "Maybe we can hang out soon?"

"Sure thing." He wraps me in a hug and kisses my forehead. "Where are you off to tonight?"

"A party?"

"I remember parties," he says. "Then you get old and go to bed at nine-thirty."

"Dad, you seriously need to have fun."

"*You* need to have fun. You're young."

"Angel, I just love spaghetti," Abby calls from her booster chair.

"Me too, Ab," I say, craning my neck to see her. She smiles sweetly, her mouth ringed with red gravy, and gives me a little wave.

chapter 10

They are cozy, Joey and Carmella. Here we are on the couch at the party's end with most everyone clearing out or already gone. I'm slumped at one end, Carmella is asleep and curled on Joey's lap in the middle, and pregnant Sherry is asleep at the other end, her head tilted back against the cushions.

Joey shifts Carmella's weight. "My shoulder fell asleep," he says. I grab her bag and jacket and hold them on my lap. She looks so trusting sprawled out against him, her dark hair falling across her cheek and her mouth sort of open. Her shirt is scrunched down a bit in the front and her bra strap shows. It's satiny blue. I fix her top, and she stirs a little but goes right on sleeping in Joey's arms.

"Taking off soon?" he asks.

I nod, but I'm not ready to wrap it up. "How's the fancy cheese these days?"

"I'm addicted," he says, shaking his head. "And getting a gut."

"Get out. And since when are you vain?"

"A gut, Angel. A gut!"

Inggy and Cork walk through the living room, Inggy hanging on Cork's shoulder. Cork barely looks at me, but Ing turns and yawns, waving goodbye. "Talk to you tomorrow."

"Yup," I say.

Joey gives Carmella a little jostle but she doesn't wake.

"Too gentle," I tell him. "Give her a poke."

"She'll get up," he says, giving her another jiggle.

"Oh, you *like* her," I tease.

"And who do you like these days?"

"Well, Sardi, I'll tell you how it is. I'm in between adventures. There's a definite lull."

"Someday," he whispers. "You'll fall for somebody."

"Maybe I fell for you," I say, growing warm all over.

He shakes his head. "I didn't feel it."

"You know how I would know if I was loved?" Sherry says from the other end of the couch. She sits up, rubs her eyes, and settles her hands on her big stomach. "If a guy carried me over a puddle. I saw that once in a movie. This girl is a skinny little thing all decked out in fierce heels, and there's this huge puddle. Her guy picks her up like she's a delicate flower and carries her over and places her down as fine as can be on the curb. To me that speaks of love." She takes a sip of Diet Coke, heaves herself off the couch, and waddles away.

Carmella stirs and yawns, gives her hair a tousle, jingling all her silver bracelets.

"You should have woke me," she says.

"It's okay," Joeys says. I hand her her bag and jacket and off they go, hand in hand.

Kipper Coleman plops down on the couch right next to me and pats my leg. "How about me and you go get a hamburger." He has good breath, like he was just eating an apple.

"What's open?"

He looks at his watch. "Shoot. Probably nothing. Not even the greasy spoon."

"I could eat a hamburger," I say.

"Oh, I wish I could make you a hamburger." He looks at me longingly. "Let me check out the fridge and I'll report back." He leaps up and sprints into the kitchen and returns a minute later with an individually wrapped slice of yellow cheese and a dill pickle on a plate. "It was the best I could do." I open the cheese and take a bite and hold it out to him but he shakes his head and says, "For you." So I eat.

"Look," Kipper says, scanning the room. "We're the pity party people, the hangers-on who don't know when to go home."

"So what?" I say. I don't want to go home yet. "Let's fox-trot."

In gym, they're teaching us ballroom dancing. Who

knows why, but honestly, it's kind of fun and interesting too. We get the fancy-schmancy handhold going, meaning your arms that aren't around each other are held rigid out to the side. Very last-century.

"Slow, slow, quick, quick," I say. "You're a good dancer, you know that?"

"You smell like a pickle."

"Sorry."

"I don't mind." He leads us around the recliner and along the coffee table. "Rock back, forward, side, together. Hey, Angel, you think I'll ever get laid?"

"Go get yourself a girlfriend."

"It's complicated," he whispers. "The ones I like don't like me and the ones I don't like don't like me either."

"Come on. Alyssa?"

"She wants to be *friends*."

"Marcie?"

"She wears Birkenstocks."

I arch an eyebrow, which I note goes very well with this arm hold.

"Don't give me that. *You* don't wear Birkenstocks." He has a point. "Am I really a good dancer?"

"Absolutely," I say. I can easily follow what he leads, and we get a real rhythm going.

"How old were you when you did it?" he asks.

"Fourteen."

"Crap. I'm so late to the game." He falls on the couch.

I want to keep dancing, but it looks like he's not moving, so I sit next to him.

He latches onto my arm. "What are the chances of you doing it with me?"

"Why me?" I shake him off.

"'Cause you're so nice, Angel. And if I touch your boob I might die on the spot. And if I can't get it up or last for like two seconds, I'm thinking you won't blab it all over." He chews on a nail. "What else could go wrong, by the way?"

"Those are the main ones, but there's also, like, bad form."

"Well, I don't have any form. Not yet anyway." He leans toward me. "I know you can't tell by looking at me, but I'm actually sexy."

"Do tell," I say, plucking a cashew from the nut bowl.

"Naked," he whispers. "I'm not so skinny, if you can believe it."

I smile into the nut bowl and brush salt from my palms and stand up. "All right."

His eyes tremble.

"I'll make out with you," I tell him.

"I'll take it."

"Don't be so grateful. It's not attractive."

"Gotcha." He leaps up and does a little hop.

"No hopping." We walk out the front door into a foggy mist.

"Can I hold your hand?"

"Yeah, okay."

"You're so pretty, Angel."

The cool, wet night swirls around us as I turn to him. "What do you like about me?"

He rakes his eyes over my face and takes about thirty seconds to answer. "It's not any one thing in particular. It's more the overall effect of your eyes, nose, mouth, and hair." I'll need to teach him something about romance. His hand is damp and warm in mine. "Let me know when we can start making out," he says.

"You're a nice guy, Kipper, but you totally need to relax."

"Don't I know it."

chapter 11

Kipper hugs his books to his chest and stands by my locker. "I adore you."

"No, you don't." I yank out my history book. He stands there staring at me, his face flushed like he has a tropical fever. "Listen," I say low. "You just need to get laid fifty more times. You need some perspective."

The bell rings, and I'm saved.

I didn't mean to. I only meant to make out on my couch. But it wasn't exactly comfy, the itchy fabric, the bad angles, and him so tall his legs hung over the edge. So I brought him upstairs and told him, "We're not doing it. It's just that I have a crick in my neck."

We made ourselves comfy and old neurotic Kipper started to relax. It turns out he never felt a boob before, at least not a naked one, so he was full of glee and spent a long time looking and touching and burying his face between my boobage, which was a nice change of pace since most guys are quick to head south. And I have to agree

Kipper is sort of sexy in a super-skinny way, *sort of* being the key words. Sexy, I guess I mean, because he was sweetly game, his face happily flushed, laughing off his mis-pokes and asking how my clit worked. When the sun started to rise and he wouldn't stop kissing my face, I finally had to throw him out.

In an Inggy-inspired moment, I take the SAT. She took it last spring and did well and she's going to see if she can beat her score, which is kind of annoying no matter how you slice it. She calls early that morning to make sure I'm awake, then picks me up in her mom's Infiniti. She's not wearing any makeup, which make her pale lashes and brows disappear, but still, she looks good, her hair swinging in an energetic ponytail.

Cork's sprawled out in the backseat, eyes closed, with a bowl of cereal on his chest. We head over to school and I'm thinking what's the point, the community college is going to take me no matter what. They have no standards. Not to mention I only went to two of the study sessions. I give her a look as we pull into the school parking lot. It's seven-forty-five a.m. on a Saturday. "Just take it," she says.

"I am," I snap.

• • •

I'm in with the first quarter of the alphabet and am sent upstairs to a large classroom along with Cork, who's still eating out of his cereal bowl. Kipper gives me a sly little wave across the room. Soon enough, the proctor, one of our grubby subs, hands out the booklets and score sheets and we begin. Oh, help me.

I didn't tell anybody, but I did bad on the PSAT. Like moron bad. What I told Inggy was that I didn't do so hot and left it at that. The thing about that stupid PSAT is that it was demoralizing. After a lot of guesses I just lost heart and could barely pay attention. I hated it, and when I hate something I just can't do it.

"Maybe standardized tests don't work for you," the old guidance counselor had said to me, glancing at my scores and my transcript littered with Cs. She took off her glasses and looked at me with ancient eyes, eyes like a turtle's. "What do you want to do with yourself, Angel?"

"I don't know."

She nodded.

"I don't love school, you know. I really can't imagine four more years."

"Maybe that's right, and maybe you'll return years later. Some do."

"You know, I don't think a job is everything. I think my

life is everything, and the job is one thing. It might be sort of interesting to be a receptionist. I'm friendly. I like people, and I like the phone. I'd like to sit at a desk and buzz people in and be the first person you see. I'm not saying I'd love it or anything, but I'd be good at it."

She focused those ancient reptilian eyes on me. "I wonder if you'd like it, but there's only one way to know. It's a start, right?"

"Right."

"Off you go," she said, patting my hand.

I sat there. "I guess no matter what plan you have life will spring surprises. I read that in a book once, about life springing its surprises. I like that. My life definitely springs things on me."

"That's true, my dear, but it doesn't mean you should wait around for what'll happen. It doesn't mean you shouldn't spring yourself."

"Right," I said, annoyed with her little maneuver, at how her words sounded better than mine.

"You'll do fine, Angel."

I nodded. "How do you think I should spring myself?"

"Hmm," she said, taking a deep breath. "Start thinking about what you want. Down the road. What matters to you."

"It's not like there's anything wrong with being a receptionist."

"Of course not. Now, off you go, because I must ske-daddle to a very boring meeting." She sighed and patted my arm. "You're a lovely girl."

I've never told anyone else my receptionist plan. Not even my mom, 'cause she would say that it pays crap. Everything pays crap in her book. And it probably would on the island, but maybe I'll move to the city. I could. Though I don't know.

11. *There is no doubt that Larry is a genuine*
    _____: *he excels at telling stories that*
    fascinate his listeners.
    a. *Braggart.* Not that, obviously.
    b. *Dilettante.* I don't remember what this means. But not this either.
    c. *Pilferer.* What the heck? Oh, pilfer. Like to lift something. Okay, not that.
    d. *Prevaricator.* What the hell. Sort of like velociraptor, but obviously not a dino-saur. No idea.
    e. *Raconteur.* Well, this I think is a word like *entrepreneur* but not. And that's like some big shot with lots of cash and a scheme, like Vic's uncle. Okay, so that's not Larry. So it has to be the di-nosaur word, but really . . . who gives a shit? Can't we just say Larry's a talker,

for God's sake? Whatever happened to plain English, and why isn't it good enough? I mean, who would say, *He sat at the table and tore into his steak like a prevaricator*? I mean, you could just say he tore into his steak. You could say he's a pig. The thing that gets me is a word should sound like what it is. Like *grimy*, for example, has a dirt feel. But a prevaricator? I mean, come on. How often am I going to work that into a sentence, even if I'm an egghead?

I stare at words, feeling myself grow damp. No, Larry is not a prevaricator. I'm certain. It must be this *raconteur*. I fill in the circle and with a pen I dig out of my bag I write both words on my hand because I'm pretty annoyed.

Then it happens. I lose heart. I fold up my answer sheet, stick it in my bag, and sit there for a while, head down, telling myself this is one small moment in my otherwise interesting life.

I get up eventually and walk out, quietly closing the door behind me, and look in through the little window at the back of the sub's head where her hairdo is crushed from sleeping on it. She's bent over a novel and everyone is hunched over their booklets. I have Cork in my line of vision, and finally he looks up and sees me. In a few seconds he lifts himself out of his seat, and I wait for him by the water fountain.

"I'm bailing," I say.

He takes my fingers and we run down two flights to the gym, so fast we're practically flying, and push through the doors. It's dark and the air is sweaty and close, and we run through the big gym into the little gym where all the mats are stacked. Cork throws me down and kisses me hard and I grab his hair and we roll around, exhilarated. I flip off my shoes, and he pushes off my jeans and underwear and my ass is on the rubber mat and we do it really hard and much too fast. I feel slammed. The best part was tearing down the stairs, flying through the gym.

"You ever do it in the gym?" he asks.

"Nope."

"Now you have."

"You?"

"Now I have." I can feel him smile. He jumps up and pulls on his jeans. It takes me longer to get everything on. "Wait," I say, but he's rushing out. "Don't go back. I can't find my sneak. Cork, my sneaker." I laugh, feeling around in the dark. He has the door open, a ray of light slivering in, but he runs back and joins my groping. "Here," he says, shoving it at me.

"I'm bailing," I say.

"You told me."

"Let's go to the beach." He takes off again, and I don't have time to put my sneaker on, so I run alongside him, one shoe on, one off, my bag bumping my hip. "Why you going back?" I say.

"Look, if you don't want to take it, don't." And he's pushing through the doors and taking the steps two at a time.

Well then. I walk out into the sunshine and take off my sneaker and walk barefoot across the street to the beach. Bye-bye, SATs. I roll up my jeans and walk near the waterline, where the wind whips my hair all around. I have to pull it back in an elastic, and while I'm in my bag I take out the score sheet. Less than a quarter filled in. How is it that this sheet can tell you how smart you are? I stare at all the hollow circles, the perfect orderly rows. And I realize there *is* an order. You start out in school and pay attention. You don't allow your mind to wander over to the window. You read what you're supposed to and write what you're supposed to and take your homework home and do it. Before a test, you study. One grade leads to the next, and step by step you learn what you need to learn. By the time you get to the SAT you naturally know what a prevaricator is because you've done things in order. I crumple up the score sheet and drop it in a garbage can on top of a potato chip bag. Sayonara.

I sit in the sand and look at the waves. God, Cork, you

could have taken a few more minutes. It wouldn't have killed you. The grubby sub was so tuned out she wouldn't have noticed how long he was gone. The sky darkens and the water changes from bluish-green to metallic gray. The wind kicks up, and the waves become foamier. Then the clouds break open, a hard rain falls, and I run like mad off the beach and across the street to the library. It's a tiny branch, and in the bathroom I wipe myself off with paper towels until I'm just damp but not soaking. I sit down in the main room to wait it out.

What is it about libraries? There's a plastic-bag lady. Lots of plastic bags filled with God knows what. She mutters and checks her watch every few seconds. There's Band-Aid man. He's got one on his chin and one on his forehead.

I find the enormous dictionary and look up *prevaricator—a person who speaks falsely*. So that's not Larry, obviously. The answer must have been that *entrepreneur* word, which is too smudged on my hand to read. So I guessed right. I fling myself into a seat, feeling wet and cold. Maybe I should have finished.

Well, I don't speak falsely. If Ing found out and came to me and said *I know*, I would never deny it. How could I? I'm no prevaricator. I think about things for a while.

The lady sitting across from me is knitting some caterpillar-like putty-colored thing. She says to her friend,

"I got the cat sprayed. I had to. If they roam outdoors you have to get them sprayed."

The friend nods.

Well, everybody's a dope, maybe, when you get right down to it. That cheers me a little.

The rain stops as suddenly as it began, and the sun comes out. As I'm leaving, a guy wipes a bench with his sweatshirt until all the beads of water are gone. He plunks down, opens a box of Yodels, rips into the plastic, and takes a happy bite. "My wife won't let me have this stuff at home. We're dieting. Want one?"

"Sure." He hands me a package and I tear into it.

A little sparrow comes along and lands right on this guy's head. Right on his head. He stops chewing and raises his eyes as if he can see up there. I burst out laughing. "There's a bird on your head," I whisper. "Crazy."

"That happened to me once before," he tells me.

What is it about his semibald, graying head that a bird has landed on it *twice*? A mystery! A very funny mystery.

The sun is shining, the Yodel is creamy chocolate deliciousness, and the little sparrow sits there for a few seconds before taking off. All this makes me feel good. It feels like a sign. Of what, I don't know.

chapter 12

The jukebox at BOWL BAR MOTEL is pretty wonderful, and so are the bowling shoes, worn down to a slippery finish and perfect for spins. So Ing and I stay in the bar dunking cheese fries in ketchup, pushing quarters into the jukebox, and dancing while the others bowl. It's a weeknight and pretty early, so we have the floor to ourselves as we groove to "Tobacco Road" and "Fever." To "Mustang Sally," one of our favorites, we pulse and grind under the dim lights and sing to each other:

> *"All you wanna do is ride around, Sally*
> *Ride, Sally, ride."*

When Joey, Carmella, and Cork come into the bar to buy snacks, "Mercy" comes on and Carmella joins us on the floor. We spin and twist and strut and shimmy. It's so nice to be a girl—to be pretty and soft with long, swinging hair. I can tell Inggy and Carmella feel it too, and our smiles flash off each other until we're deep inside the music, moving with it, feeling it pulse like a heartbeat. We must be good to watch. Joey leans against the bar with a basket of onion rings, and Cork sits on a stool waiting for his order. I can feel their eyes on me.

When the song ends, Carmella snuggles close to Joey and nibbles on an onion ring. Soon she heads to the bathroom, and I walk up and pluck a ring from his basket.

"That was good dancing," he says.

"It feels good." I look into his shy eyes.

"'Walk by the spirit, and you will not gratify the desires of the flesh,'" an old lady eating chicken wings at the bar cries. "'For the desires of the flesh are against the spirit, and the desires of the spirit are against the flesh.'"

"Shut it, hag," Cork says, joining Inggy on the bench.

"Hey." Joey turns to chicken-wing lady. "Did you know the Bible's got sexy parts?"

"Blasphemy!" she says, sucking on the greasy meat.

"For real?" I ask him.

"Song of Songs. Read it."

"I will."

"I'm not mad at you, Angel."

"Huh?"

"I keep meaning to tell you," he says in a low voice. "From when we were together . . ."

"Why aren't you mad at me?" I'm confused, and this isn't what I want to ask. I grab another onion ring.

"You gonna eat my whole basket?"

I take a bite. "I think you're a little mad."

"Nope." He walks away, and it can't be good what he's telling me.

He, Carmella, and Cork go back to the lanes and the Bible-spouting chicken-wing-eating lady leaves and Inggy and I dance some more until we're sweaty and pooped. Inggy stretches out on the duct-tape-patched bench and admires her bowling shoes, turning them this way and that. I tell her what Joey said about Song of Songs.

"I'm definitely gonna look that up," she says.

"You and me both. Hey, Ron," I call to the owner as he collects empties off the bar. "You have Bibles in the rooms?"

"Has the spirit moved you?"

After some serious coaxing, he gives us a key and we skitter across the parking lot, the asphalt glimmering under the neon BOWL BAR MOTEL sign, and climb a staircase to one of the rooms.

In the desk drawer, we find a Bible, and Inggy flips through the pages till she finds it. We settle on the scratchy bedspread and take turns reading aloud. Right off the bat the woman wants to be kissed "with the kisses of his mouth." The man tells her her boobs are like two fawns. She and he spend a lot of time comparing each other's body parts to ripe fruit and whatnot—wine, anointing oils, henna blossoms, nectar. They're swoony, these two.

"'Your cheeks are like halves of a pomegranate,'" I read. "You know just what he's talking about."

"Dang," Inggy says.

She runs her finger under a line. "'I am my beloved's and his desire is for me.' She's bold, for sure."

I nod. There's no doubt she's a horndog, this sister of Israel. She "seeks him" and tells him to "make haste." I like that—make haste—and will find a way to work it into conversation.

"Cork and I," Inggy says. "We did it at school." She lets out a laugh and covers her mouth.

"You did?" I turn to her. "Where?"

"In the old art room. During study hall. On one of the tables."

"So tell me," I say, getting a little itchy and jealous.

"I want to tell you something else."

"What?" I say, carefully.

She closes the Bible and lies back on the pillow and tells me this story:

Just recently she was on the campus of one of the good schools she applied to and had some wadded-up garbage in her hand. Usually a good aim, she missed the can and it landed next to a guy lounging on the grass. He heroically picked it up and brought it over and told her to try again. This time she sank it. It was very satisfying, she said, getting to try again.

He was eating a swiss cheese sandwich, this guy, and reading a little book of poems. "For a class?" Ing wanted to know. "For me," he said. She liked that—"for me." They talked. He wasn't exactly cute, though not uncute, and appealing in some indefinable way. He was on the small side and slouchy but comfortable in his slouchiness. And he had a steady gaze, not creepy steady, but like you had his attention. He read her a poem about the happiness of sitting in a dense leafy tree during a rainstorm. She borrowed his pen to write the poem's name on her hand. He wanted to take her to a party that night and said it like they'd known each other for a long time. Inggy wanted to go, but she and her parents were leaving that day. He told her she should come to the school next year, that it was a good place, mostly as good as the hype.

Her parents were sitting on a bench, frantically waving her over. Her dad had bought hot knishes and could not abide a cold knish. But she couldn't move away. Instead she asked how he would spend his afternoon, because she liked imagining the rest of his day. "I'll probably think some thoughts," he said. She felt herself grow warm in a good way. She pointed out to him that it's very hard to say something like that and not sound like a wiseass. She told him he sounded sort of true. "I am sort of true," he said, simply. He took her hand and held it for a minute, each of them feeling perfectly understood.

Inggy inches close to me on the bed. "I kept thinking

about the conversation and I realized something." She hooks her hair behind her ears and gets a serious look. "I'm not sure this makes sense, so bear with me. But I realized we're turning out. I mean, we can't see how we're turning out because it happens so infinitesimally, but we are. It made me realize that when I go off to school, I'll get to find out—" Then she looks at me, me who won't be going off to school. "I mean, when we graduate and get away from all these morons we've known forever, we'll really get a chance to see who we've become. Meanwhile a stranger comes along and I get a glimpse of myself. I liked the girl he saw, so I decided to *really* be her. Did you notice anything?"

I shake my head, and she looks flustered.

"Well, I feel different, a little, anyway, and Cork must feel it too. Things are more exciting with him lately. We did it in the old art room! I was sure he sensed something in me." She looks at me hopefully, and I should agree. I should nod.

"Probably," I say, then add, "but maybe he just wanted to spice things up."

"Maybe."

We're quiet for a minute. I pull her over to the mirror, and we share the desk chair and give ourselves a good look under the dim light. She glows a little, pale and pink, with blue eyes as clear as a sky. Her silky hair falls in a sheet down her back. Me, I'm the opposite. Dark eyes, dark curly hair, olive skin. We look at ourselves and each other. I reach for her hand on the desk and rub it, feeling the delicate bones and the small swell of blue veins and wonder what it means to be Inggy inside that long stretch of white skin. Is she different, has she changed, and have I missed it?

"You like being pretty, Angel?"

"Uh-huh."

"I read that Marilyn Monroe said it's a burden. Sometimes I think I know what she meant."

"I might leave New Jersey, you know. I just might," I say, touching my face.

"I've never slept with anyone but Cork," she says with wonder.

"Well, you will."

"I guess that's right." Her eyes tear up.

"You didn't tell me any of this, Ing." I have no right, but I say it anyway. "You've had all this stuff going on inside you."

"It's been a jumble in my head."

"It's okay," I say. "So this guy, this slouchy guy with the undefinable something, did you want to do it with him?" I slip an arm around her and she tips her white head against mine. "Of course you did," I tell her.

"How will I ever leave Cork?"

"They'll be new guys, lots of guys. The guys will come and go, but it's friendship that lasts."

"But how will I ever leave him?" She stares at her reflection as if it knows the answer.

"How will you ever leave me?"

Inggy startles, and I guess I do too. "Leave you? You'll visit me," she says. "I'll come home. We'll talk on the phone, text. . . ."

"Oh, I know, I know."

"With Cork everything will have to be different. . . . I do love him." She blinks away her tears. "Say something, Angel."

But I can't. Maybe I'm too filled with secrets. Am I a bad person? It doesn't feel bad. Not really. It's separate, me and Cork. And it doesn't mean anything. If Inggy found out would she see that I'm still me and we're still us? I think so. I really do.

Joey, though, would lose all faith. He expects too much. Maybe you can't expect so much. Joey feels lost to me forever.

chapter 13

Just one more time, or two. Then I'll stop. But it's Friday, and the night awaits me. Mom's having a party, Inggy's at some Journalists of Tomorrow seminar in DC, and my immediate prospects are Kipper or Cork. Need I say more.

Kipper's writing me notes these days, folding them a million times and slipping them into my locker. *Friday, Oct. 14, 1:16 p.m.: Let's go on a date tonight! A movie? A stromboli on the boardwalk? We could fox-trot. Full moon tonight! p.s. I'm not looking to get laid. p.s.2 But if you want to, great! p.s.3 Maybe you'll let me hold your hand in any case.*

After school, Cork stops by my locker as I'm looking in a tiny mirror I taped to the door. I can only see my mouth as I rub on lip gloss. "I'll come over later," he whispers.

"All right," my glossy mouth says.

• • •

I heat up a Hot Pocket while Mom backs out of the refrig-erator with an armful of guacamole, salsa, cheddar cheese, olives, and hummus. The kids are with TB, who has not been invited to this party of hers tonight. "How do I look, by the way?" she asks.

"Can I run a chip through that?" I reach for the tub of guac.

"Go ahead." She hands it off. "Good?" she says, twirling.

"You're smokin' but simple." I crunch a chip. She has on a black halter dress and sleek midheel wedges. Her hair waves nicely around her face. Definitely sexy but low-key tonight. It's a good look for her and probably has some-thing to do with the banker she's been dating.

I take a long bike ride into the state park. The moon is indeed full, and it's a bright, cold night. The island is so different in the off-season. There are some lingering ben-nies on the weekends in September, but slowly the place clears out and by October it's quiet, quiet, quiet. I ride along the dunes until I get tired and then take a walk on the beach. It's windy and deserted; I'm not dressed warm enough and start to shiver, but I like the night beach. The full moon. The moonlit sand, the waves silvery in the brightness. Nature is sexy, and that makes me think God is alive and has very good taste. I can go a long time without thinking about God, but then I do, and tonight God is this beach. And wouldn't you know, I see a little fox up on the dunes. You don't see them often, but there it is, its eyes sparks of light. When I'm shivering too much, I hurry back to my bike.

I'm cold and sweaty when I get back home. My mom's party is in full swing, cars parked all over, the house lit up, and music humming through the walls. I walk my bike over the stones to the shed. Cork sits waiting on the back stoop of the Corner House.

"Where've you been?" he says, a little pissed.

"Out and about."

Upstairs, I take off my clothes, leave them in a heap, and head for the shower. "Wanna join me?"

"No," he says. But a few minutes later he pulls back the shower curtain and watches me soap up, his eyes never leaving me. It's juicy, him holding back. Finally he peels off his T-shirt, unzips and drops his pants, and joins me under the steamy water. We do it sitting in the tub with a drizzle of water falling over us. After, I plug the drain and let it fill, and we lounge for a while, Cork's long legs climbing the tile.

"Do you think God's sexy?" I ask.

"Hell no."

"Explain."

"What kind of a Catholic are you, Cassonetti?"

"I'm not really. I went to church a few times with my

grandma when I was little. I liked the smells. What is it? Wax and incense and something else? I liked the stained glass and the candles. I liked the general mood when no one was talking."

"Well, if you spent any real time in a church you wouldn't think God is sexy, and especially not if you went to catechism."

"That's a shame."

"But I'll tell you what is sexy. This ass." He slides his hands under my butt and squeezes. "This is one delicious ass and this is one fine tit," he says, cupping my boob.

"God made this ass and boob," I say, and laugh.

"Yeah, good one."

I'd like to ask him about sex in the old art room. On the table. But I never talk with him about the private stuff Inggy tells me. It wouldn't be right.

I wake around two as Cork is putting on his clothes. "Bye," he says.

"Bye."

I toss and turn for a while. Mom's party must have wound down, 'cause I don't hear music anymore. I feel kind of restless, both tired and antsy. Not a good combination. I wouldn't mind some cheese or something, so I throw on jeans and a sweatshirt and dash over to the House in my slippers. When I open the back door, in the dimly lit kitchen Cork is kissing my mom against the refrigerator. They pull apart and look at me, and I look at them.

"Ew," I say.

On the table is a half-eaten cheese tray, the slices nicely arranged in a semicircle. I grab a couple and leave.

The back door opens, and I hear her slowly climb the stairs. She kicks off her wedges and leans on the doorframe. She puts one bare foot on top of the other and leans there like a girl. My mother is a girl. She tosses me a napkin full of cheese slices and some jump out and land on the sheets.

"Say something!"

She shrugs, sighs, and then she laughs. She actually laughs, covering her mouth and shaking her head. "Oh, Angel, I'm sorry."

"You kissed a seventeen-year-old! What is wrong with you?" I throw a pillow at her and it clips her in the face before she catches it.

"I am such an ass," she says.

"You really are!"

"I can't even explain."

I try to get my brain around this. My mom. Ew. My mom! I grab a cheese slice and chew it slowly, filling my mouth with sharpness. Cork cheated on me. On me and Inggy both. There must be others too, I now know as surely as I know I am sitting on this bed. Cork is suddenly and absolutely a stranger to me, and so is my mother.

"Look," she says. "What can I say . . . ?"

"I don't know! But you better say something."

She sits on the bed and gathers up the scattered slices and stacks them on the napkin.

"Get off." I slap the bed. But she sinks down on the pillow and rubs her face like she's really tired. She's wearing a lot of rings, and I've never noticed before, but her hands, decked with all those rings, are old-looking, dry with a million tiny lines.

"Did he start it up? Did he?" I move to the window ledge and lean against it.

"He's a flirt, that one," she says. "Look, it was nothing. It didn't look like nothing but it was nothing. One too many mojitos and a horny boy aren't a good recipe. Let's forget it, all right?" Then she bursts out laughing and covers her mouth, looking a little bit shocked. When she recovers, she says, "I am sooo sorry. But you know, Cork and Inggy are ridiculous. Being exclusive all these years. You're kids, for god's sake. Has he ever hit on you?"

"Of course not!"

"Well, I'll tell you, Cork's got a lot of living in him."

"Yeah, you think? He's seventeen." And an asshole.

"That's not what I meant."

"I know what you meant."

"There's love, Angel, and there's sex. And there's a whole lot more sex than love."

"I already know that." I sit on the bed and poke at the cheese, and when she reaches for a slice I pull the napkin away.

"Come on," she says gently. She dangles her ringy hand in front of me.

"What smells good?" I say. "What is that?"

"Coco." She holds out a wrist. "It's nice, right?"

"Why can't you find anyone? Why are you always looking?"

She gets up and looks at herself in the wall mirror, running her hands through her hair. "Maybe when you're ready it finds you. Maybe I'm not ready."

"What are you waiting for?"

"I don't know," she says, getting annoyed. "Relationships are work, Angel. Maybe that's why your old mother is alone. Maybe I'm too selfish."

"God, I can't believe you!" I replay it in my mind. "You and— Ew!"

"Look, Inggy doesn't need to know any of this. Not that you'd tell her, but trust me, the Inggys of the world especially don't need to know these things."

"Am I selfish?"

"You're a teenager. You're supposed to be. But you're kind, Angel. You are."

I look out at the bay. The water is dark and smooth, and

126

the cattails ripple in the wind. All is right with the world out there, but in here it is perfectly wrong. I know one thing: when I'm Mom's age I'm going to know when to stop being a girl. "What happened to the banker?"

"Didn't come. Something about the babysitter being sick." She shrugs. "I'll see you in the morning." And she heads down the stairs, dangling her shoes in her hands.

"What did you mean, the Inggys of the world don't need to know these things?" I call after her.

But she doesn't answer.

chapter 14

The next morning a low fog hangs over the bay. I stay in bed for a long time, dozing on and off, then finally rise and take a long, hot shower, scrubbing myself very clean.

And then I'm saved.

As I pull on jeans, Mossy pokes his head in the back door and yells, "Your dad's on the phone." I jog over to the House with wet hair to find out that Ginger's mother's ulcer is acting up, so Ginger's off to Egg Harbor for a few days. "Come have dinner with us," my dad says. Better yet, I tell him, I'll hang out and help him with the girls. So it's set. I eat a cold piece of French toast from a plate on the counter and tell everybody I'm leaving as I lick my sticky fingers.

"I wanna come," Mimi says.

Mom sits at the kitchen table, hunched over her checkbook with no makeup on and her hair in a low, sloppy ponytail. She glances at me quickly, smiles, adjusts her reading glasses. "For a few days, huh?"

"Yup." I pour myself a splash of orange juice. "Bye, little man," I say to Mossy, who's curled up the couch in front of the TV. He holds up his hand, and I give him five.

"I wanna come." Mimi follows me to the door.

"Ride your bike over later," I say, cupping her head.

I pack a bag, throwing in a toothbrush, mascara, jeans, underwear, and a couple of shirts, and then I am outta there.

It's nice hanging out with my dad. The first night he cooks a big Italian meal, and we take the kids to the A & P and load up the cart with a lot of stuff Ginger wouldn't approve of, I'm sure. After dinner I give the girls a bath, and naked and slippery, they dash down the hall and I chase them. I love their bright little faces, their wet eyelashes. When I tuck Abby in, she puts her sleepy arms around my neck. "Oh, isn't this nice? I want you to come live with me. You can sleep right here," she says, patting the space next to her.

Cork and I—we don't say a word to each other at school or anywhere else. Inggy's out sick on Monday after her Journalists of Tomorrow weekend, so Cork and I keep a good distance.

• • •

That night Dad suggests we go out to dinner, and we have another feast, seafood this time, which is clearly not in the Ginger budget. After the girls are in bed, I sit with him on the couch and tell him my receptionist plan.

"Maybe I could, you know, even live in the city."

He sinks down into the cushions and thinks about it. "The city's not cheap, and that kind of job isn't going to pay you much."

"Well, you gotta start somewhere."

"You could take a few business classes at Ocean Community."

"I guess."

"Hey," he says. "You know Tom at the marina with the fifty-foot Albemarle? He's a big shot at some financial firm in downtown Manhattan. We can ask him about a job for you this summer."

"Financial firm, huh? Could that be a snore?" But somehow I'm feeling pretty okay about this.

"Well, honeybunch, you'd be doing the meeting and greeting, not the calculating."

"True." It sorta feels like a plan.

• • •

Inggy, I have to say, is one of these annoying people who will come to school sick. So on Tuesday she's back, stuffed-up and watery-eyed and sneezing, and the three of us talk before homeroom, as usual.

Cork: Get this, a twenty-foot shark in
      Australia bit a guy in half as he was
      snorkeling.
Inggy: Holy crap, what happens when you
      get bit in half?
Cork: You die instantly.
Me: Which half? From the top down or
      bottom up?
Cork: Bottom up.
Inggy: At least he didn't see it coming.
      Achoo!
Me: Yay to that. Bless you.

But when we're alone, not one word passes between me and Cork. And I have to give this a think. Doesn't he feel the need to say something? Anything? Sorry, even? But no, nothing. So I corner him after science. Get right in his face and stare him down. But he only lowers his eyes and slinks away.

● ● ●

The last night I spend at my dad's we sit on barstools at the counter and have a beer. How often do I have a beer with my dad? Never.

"I'm glad Ginger's mom has an ulcer," I say.

"Me too." He smiles, knocking bottles with me. "I don't get to see you enough."

"Are you happy, Dad?"

"Yes, certainly," he says, too quickly. Personally, I think this is a question that requires some thought. "I have three beautiful girls, the marina, fishing, my boat, Ginger. You happy?"

I smile.

"What's wrong?"

"Nothing." We're quiet, and it's nice being on side-by-side stools. "Sometimes I wish I could figure out stuff."

"You know," he says, "when I was young I thought there'd come a time when I'd feel like a grown-up, when things would click. And it's true you figure out stuff the older you get, but there's always confusing, utterly baffling crap-a-doodle-doo. Sometimes you still feel like the kid who knows diddly-squat. The kid with a finger up his nose who's going 'Huh?' "

"Comforting, Dad."

"Hey, you asked."

"Mom still thinks she's a teenager."

"She's still looking, your mother."

132

"For a guy?"

"Yeah, that and other stuff." ·

"Why'd you split? I mean, I know you were young and all, and fighting, but why really?"

He shrugs. "'Cause we both had our fingers up our noses going 'Huh?' And technically a relationship can't handle both of you going 'Huh?' at the same time."

"What pearls of wisdom."

"Your old dad's a wise one."

I peel the wet label off my beer. "Hey, why doesn't Ginger like me?"

He sighs and kisses me on the side of the head. "I don't know."

"Come on."

"I like you."

Wednesday, in gym, we dance the fox-trot and the cha-cha. Inggy, still sick and wearing her glasses and looking all foggy-eyed, sits it out in the bleachers with a pack of tissues. Kipper comes gliding over to take my hand, but Cork cuts in and grabs me first. "What are you doing?" I say as his fingers close over mine. Soon we're fox-trotting around the gym, passing Inggy on every rotation. I feel Cork's eyes on me so I stare back dead on. He doesn't seem the least bit sorry or embarrassed; instead he looks like he wants to say something and is scrambling to find words. When the song slows he lets us fall behind so we're barely moving. He opens his mouth.

I say, "Just shut the fuck up, Cork."

I'll give him this—he does.

Back at home, Mom's at the sewing machine making Mimi a costume. Mimi stands in front of me in a blond wig that touches her butt. "What are you supposed to be?" I ask.

"The Little Mermaid," Mossy says, walking through the living room in a zombie getup.

"The Little Mermaid is for like three-year-olds! I'm a *sexy* mermaid!" She holds two clamshells to her flat chest and says, "Fierce. Check me out."

"Oh brother," Mossy says. The phone rings and he wanders into the kitchen to answer it.

"Cool," I say. "But what's gonna hold up those clamshells?"

"Glue."

"A flesh-colored bodysuit," Mom says.

"No bodysuit!" Mimi says.

Mom stops sewing. "You're wearing the bodysuit."

Mossy lurches in with zombie arms and tells Mimi, "It's your stupid boyfriend."

"Which one?"

"JJ."

"I haven't decided if I like him yet," she says, fluffing up her wig and scampering into the kitchen.

"That child." Mom takes her foot off the pedal and smiles at me through her glasses. "So, nice visit?"

"Yup."

"Good. Hold this for me, will you?" I pull up a chair and hold a strip of sequins as she sews them onto the leggings. Her stitching is amazingly straight. She inspects her work and then turns to me. "So hi, Angel," she says nicely.

"Hey yourself."

"I made gnocchi for tonight."

"Good." I'm not in the mood for the buttering-up routine.

She cuts a new row of sequins and says in a low voice, "So it turns out the banker really did have babysitter trouble. I'm going to see him this week." She shrugs.

"I'm glad, Ma." And I sorta am.

Mossy lurches over and puts his hands around my neck. "See my chewed-up brains?" He looks at me with glee. "They ooze out of my head and spill over my ear."

"Perfect." I finger his rubber brain.

"Ha!" Mimi says from the kitchen. "I might not even like you!"

"Don't be a snot-nose," Mom yells.

Mossy lurches off, practicing his zombie walk.

Mom catches my eye, a small smile creeping onto her face as she shakes her head. "Can you believe your old mother is so dumb?" she whispers.

"I'm not gonna be so dumb."

She laughs. "Oh, you think so, do you? Just wait, kiddo. You'll do dumb things too."

"Not like that, I won't."

She peers at me over the tops of her glasses. "I'm sorry," she snaps. "I'm sorry. What else can I say!"

chapter 15

On Halloween, Inggy and I sit in the loft of the lifeguard house, dangling our legs over the edge and watching the party below. Some of the girls are dressed up but none of the guys are. I'm wearing Mimi's dirty white boa around my neck, and false eyelashes. Ing has a silk scarf wrapped around her head and an eye patch over one eye, and a hilarious skinny mustache drawn on with eyeliner.

"Beer run!" someone yells.

Ing and I dig through our bags and come up with a bunch of singles, which she runs downstairs. Her bag is spilled open, and as I put her lip gloss, wallet, and sunglasses back in, I take a quick peek at her text messages. Nothing from Cork, one from me, one from her mom, and one from Jeffrey. Who's this Jeffrey? It says, "Hope you didn't catch the communal cold." Well, she definitely did, Jeffrey, and did she get it from you? Would Inggy cheat? More likely she caught it sitting in some egghead seminar with germy Jeffrey. But why no mention of this Jeffrey guy? And why *Jeffrey*, not Jeff?

Through the glass doors I can see Cork sitting on the stoop outside, and I wonder what he's thinking. His hood's up and pointy. Sherry, huger than ever—she can't even button her coat—slowly lowers herself between him and Tank-Top Tony.

Inggy climbs the stairs with a pumpkin bucket of candy corn, which she's shoveling into her mouth. "So yummy," she says. "I'm gonna rot my teeth out of my head."

Kipper climbs halfway up the ladder. "Can I join you?"

"Only if you take this away from me."

"Gimme," he says, waving his hand. "What can I bring you instead? Name it."

"How about a cupcake," I say. "White bottom, chocolate top."

"Chocolate bottom, white top for me," Inggy says.

"And two beers," I add.

"Coming right up," he says, scurrying down the ladder.

Inggy giggles. "He's gonna make a dancing girl happy someday."

"I'll tell you a secret." I bump shoulders with her. "I did it with him."

She laughs. "Yeah, right."

"I did," I whisper.

She flips up her eye patch and looks at me.

"It sorta happened."

"How does that sorta happen?"

It does, I want to explain. *It does sorta happen*. The thing is, Inggy knows about some of the guys I've been with, but I don't tell her everything. It's okay with me, though, if she knows this, so I give her a recap of the Kipper rendezvous.

"Oh my," she says. "Kipper Coleman."

I shrug.

"Was it . . . fun?"

"Sorta kinda. I think he's finally gotten the hint that, you know, it's not going anywhere."

"Just once, then."

"Just once."

"I can't believe you!" She laughs. "Well, dang. Kipper got laid! You made him a happy man, no doubt."

"I did."

"Sometimes you surprise me, Angel."

"Why?"

She pulls off some cobweb from the railing and lets it float down into the living room. "You have to stop."

I snap my head toward her. "Stop what?"

She puts her hand on my leg. "Could I be drunk on candy corn? Is that possible?" She lies back in the loft.

"It's totally possible. I want to hear more about your weekend."

"I told you."

"Only the boring parts."

"There were definitely boring parts."

"Come on," I say. "Did you make some friends?"

So then she tells me about two girls, one from Virginia, the other from Connecticut, Chrissy and Kate, and the life and death of the newspaper seminar, and journalism's future, and she's putting me to sleep. No mention of Jeffrey. I give her a poke. "What were the guys like?"

"Fine. A few overly earnest types." She smiles and yawns. Is she not going to say, or is there really nothing to say?

"What do you mean I have to stop?"

She turns to me. *"Kipper?"*

"You make him sound like head lice."

She shakes her head. "I only mean that you don't want him, so what were you doing?"

"But it wasn't a big deal. It was friendly. You know. The worst part was him getting all moony afterwards."

She sticks her finger in the hot wax of a candle and it hardens over her nail. "Sex is kind of a big deal, if you ask me."

"Well, it depends. And you can lose the attitude."

"Yeah, okay." We're quiet. She rolls the wax over her finger and into a ball. "Just be choosier, Angel. That's all I'm saying."

Kipper climbs the ladder, carefully balancing two plastic cups of beer and two cupcakes. "Am I good or am I good?" he says.

"You're good," Inggy says with the littlest smirk, and I totally regret telling her.

That's when the party stops being fun. At the end of the night Inggy's on one side of the couch and Cork's on the other and their legs are tangled together. I catch Cork's eye and he looks away, which pisses me off, because if anyone's gonna look away it's gonna be me. Sherry's in the recliner, holding her belly and drinking Diet Coke, and Carmella's sitting on the arm of the chair eating Mallomars and wearing bunny ears. I wander into the kitchen and pick up a cupcake and lick at the blue icing.

Cork comes in pretty buzzed and leans against the sink and watches. I chuck the bald cupcake into the trash.

"Hey, you," he says.

"Shut it, Cork."

"Come on," he whispers. "Come on, Angel." I give him the finger and walk out.

Everybody's yawning, but no one wants to leave yet. Why is that? It's late, the conversation's thin, the beer's drunk, the cupcakes are picked over, but still, no one wants to pack it in. Joey, Kipper, Tony, and I play darts, and I win by a hair. When no one's looking Joey slaps me on the butt. We play another round, and then Carmella says, "Joe, let's hit it." We all head out into the night. The wind roars.

I'm feeling a little philosophical. There's Inggy, my best friend, with her hand in Cork's. And there's Joey, my Joey, with his hand in Carmella's. It's very complicated, which is what life is, and here's the living proof. I huddle in my jacket, wishing for a hand to hold. I catch up to Sherry and nudge her. "How you feeling?"

"I seriously have gas." Well, what is a person to say?

"Christ," Tony says. I hold the door open while she heaves herself behind the wheel and Tony gets in the other side and slams his door.

Inggy looks back as a big gust whips her hair over her head. "Hurry, Angel," she laughs as she and Cork run to her dad's car. But I walk over to Kipper, who's behind the wheel of his mom's lime-green Fiesta. I knock on the window. "Can I have a ride?"

"Sure."

I wave in Inggy's direction and climb in the Kipper-mobile, which smells like cough drops.

"So this is just a ride home, right? 'Cause I'm no good at innuendo. So if this is more you should let me know so that I'm not going to be tortured with anticipation."

"It takes five minutes to drive me home. You're going to be tortured for five minutes?"

"I will."

"Oh, Kipper. I just want a ride." I watch his face crumple like a kid's. I squeeze his arm. "I'm really not available, you know."

"Come on, you are so."

"I do have a life beyond high school," I tell him.

"See, that's so cool, because I totally don't. How do you manage that?"

I smile. "*Innuendo*. What a good word. I'm going to find a way to work that into conversation."

"I'll remind you."

Kipper's quiet and drives like an old lady. Even though there isn't much traffic he comes to a full stop at a stop sign and looks both ways before moving ahead.

"Safety first," I joke, and he gives me a quick smile.

He pulls in front of my house and looks at me sweetly, shyly. "Here you are."

"S'okay. This isn't innuendo. You wanna come up? Just this time?"

chapter 16

That Friday, Cork's parents are off to Atlantic City for the night. When Ing calls to tell me that the plan is to hang out at his place, I say I have a stomachache.

"We're just going to hang out on the couch. Come."

"I don't think so."

"You're not mad at me, are you?" I'm surprised she asks; we've avoided talking about Kipper all week.

"That wasn't too nice, Ing."

"Telling you to be choosier?"

"Yeah."

"I can't tell my best friend to be choosier?"

"Do I tell you what to do?"

"Why can't I tell you what I think?"

"Why are you judging me? Okay, so you wouldn't sleep with Kipper Coleman. You made that crystal-clear. But just because you wouldn't—"

"Whoa there. For the record, I think Kipper's cute in an indescribably goofy way."

"In an indescribably goofy super-skinny way." We laugh.

"Right," she says. "But—"

"But what?"

"You're not gonna date him."

"So what?"

"It's just disingenuous, that's all. I mean, why bother? Why not sleep with someone you care about?"

"Disingenuous?"

"Well, sorta," she says, her voice getting high.

"There's no one I'm interested in at the moment."

"Okay. Just come to Cork's. Come have your stomach-ache over here."

"I don't think so. I'll call you tomorrow." I hang up.

Disingenuous? I think that means "not real." I go over to the House and get the Webster's off the shelf, and sure enough, it means "insincere." Sitting on the floor, I think about that. I'm pretty sure Kipper wouldn't say I'm disingenuous.

I deep-condition my mop with my mom's fancy-schmancy conditioning oil and sit with a plastic bag on my head to keep the heat in as I channel flip. Mom's out with the banker and the kids are with TB, so it's me and the TV. As I rinse the conditioner out, I think about maybe drying my hair and riding over to Cork's, but instead I stay up late watching TV and snacking. Then I go to my house, put on my leopard-print nightie, and lie on my bed wide awake. Around one o'clock I get dressed and bike over to 7-Eleven for a hot chocolate. While I'm fiddling with the chocolate packet, this guy named Danny walks in. He graduated a couple of years ago and goes to the community college and works in the deli at the A & P. He owns a small Grady-White and fills his tank at the marina.

"You're up late," he says, tearing open a package of Ring Dings with his teeth.

"Hey," I say. "You too." He's a pretty quiet guy, but cute in a look-twice kind of way, meaning the more you look the better he becomes, which is really an interesting phenomenon if you think about it.

"You need a ride?"

"My bike," I say, pointing outside. I stir in hot water and add a splash of milk. "How've you been?"

We talk for a minute and then he says, "We should have pizza sometime."

"I like pizza."

"Okay then." He takes my number and pays for his Ring Dings and leaves.

That could be fun. I sit on the curb out front and sip my drink. It's good and hot and the air is chilly without being too cold. Then I get the idea to visit Joey. He might be up, depending on when he got back from Cork's. I walk the couple of blocks to his house, sipping my drink and missing him again. I don't think Joey would call me disingenuous either.

I walk to the back of the house to his window, which is cracked, and call, "Hey, Joey, you up?" The window raises and there stands Carmella with tousled hair, wearing a football jersey.

"Oh," I blurt.

She tilts her head. "Hey."

"Sorry, I didn't mean to wake you guys." I cringe.

"I was up." She thumbs toward the bed. "But this guy is sound asleep."

"Yeah." I look into the half darkness at Joe stretched on the bed under a sheet. "Anyway, I'm not stalking. I swear. Just couldn't sleep. I'll get going."

"Stay." She shrugs, grabs her bag, and lights up a cigarette. "He hates when I smoke." She blows a stream out the window. "You used to smoke, right? A long time ago?"

"A really long time ago. Like four years. But I got the patch."

She nods. "Maybe I should try. You don't crave one?"

"I like watching. I'll watch you smoke." I grab the wobbly stool from behind the shed and carry it over. And it is nice watching her take a drag and shoot the cool stream into the night air. "Did you guys go to Cork's?"

She shakes her head. "We saw a movie, went to Fat Sal's for a slice, and came back here and went at it for like seven whole minutes before he falls straight asleep. We're like an old married couple, I swear." She takes a deep drag on her cigarette. "Why can't you sleep?"

I shrug. "Sometimes I just can't."

"High school bores the crap out of me."

"I'm not bored, exactly."

She leans on the sill and cups her chin in her hand, the cigarette jutting from her fingers glamorously. "Isn't it funny how some guys are such shits? They can totally live without you and let you know like every second. Then there are guys who glom on. Joey's a bit of a glommer."

I nod.

"You can't win."

I wave a finger between her and sleeping Joey. "Are you—"

"Am I gonna break up with him?" She stubs out her cigarette and looks at me coolly. "Probably not. I want a date to the prom. You have to plan ahead, and it's so lame to drag a college boy. Like they want to go. Plus, he's a nice guy, Joe." She yawns. "And a glommer's better than a shit."

"It's true."

"I'm in a funk. I went to see my grandma today in the nursing home. She's lost it. Oh, my poor granny!" She digs in her bag for a tissue. "So we sit out in the garden and she mostly doesn't have a clue what's going on, but she's still sorta herself. She still likes Fritos." She blows into the tissue. "And there's this old man on his little motor cart and he just rides in a circle, making loop after loop. Loop after loop. The whole time we're sitting there I thought I'd have to kill myself." She takes a package of Starbursts out of her bag and offers me one.

I laugh.

"What? That was funny?"

"You have the most amazing bag." I pinch out a cherry one and unwrap it.

"I know, right?" She uncrinkles one and pops it in her mouth.

"I miss my grandma too," I say.

"Oh, my little granny!"

"Mine made the best gravy."

"There's nothing like a grandma."

"There really isn't."

Carmella dabs her eyes with a tissue. "We have good stuff to look forward to. We do," she says, the Starburst bulging in her cheek. "Like Miss Merry Christmas. We'll get nominated. You and me and Inggy. Of course, Inggy'll probably win. . . ."

"Christmas!" I say.

"It'll be here before you know it." It seems so far off, but yeah, she's right. Every year the senior class nominates four pretty girls and the town votes. All the girls ride on a float in the Christmas parade, but the winner sits high on top of the float wearing a crown. And she gets a hundred bucks.

"I should get going," I say. I look in at Joe curled on his

side. "It's hard, isn't it? You break up with someone and then you can't know them anymore."

"I don't always want to know them after I ditch 'em."

"I do," I say. "Sometimes, at least."

"Well . . ."

"I didn't mean to butt in."

"Be his friend, by all means. I can't be his *everything*." She takes a pocket mirror from her bag and gives herself a once-over.

"Carmella," I say, "what do you think it is about Inggy? That she'll win?"

She yawns, blowing fruity Starburst and cigarette breath my way. "She's got that *thing*. But," she says, digging in her bag for another cigarette, then pointing it at me, "I'll give her a run for her money." She lights up, and smoke curlicues above our heads.

I jog back to 7-Eleven and my bike. The moon is bright in the dark sky, and I'm nice and warm inside my hoodie, my breath coming out in little clouds. Miss Merry Christmas. They'll take our pictures and hang them all over town. Next to interest rates, pizzas, calzones, and *Super Savers*. Everyone will vote and crown a winner. . . .

Inggy's beautiful, true. Cool and blue-eyed and queenly. Maybe that crown would look right on her head. Maybe beauty trumps sexy. In theory it does. Beauty is better, I admit. But sexy is the body. It's the eyes. It's electric. It's willing. I look at myself in the chrome of the doors of 7-Eleven. My long, curly hair blows all around my face and the 7-Eleven sign shines brightly in the reflection. There are lots of guys who might vote for me. I could win. Maybe.

chapter 17

In World Problems, Mrs. Crisp is talking about the Middle East when Sherry's water breaks and trickles under her desk. "Shit," Sherry cries, heaving herself up. "People, I'm having a baby."

"Holy crap!" someone yells.

"Ew," the kid sitting next to her says, inching his desk away.

Sherry clutches her stomach. "Shouldn't I, like, feel something?"

Mrs. Crisp looks annoyed and then hurries over, sees the little puddle, and escorts her to the office. "Angel, tell Tony," Sherry yells from the hall.

I hustle to the gym, where the boys are playing basketball, and wave Tony over. "Her water broke."

"What am I supposed to do?" He's for real. He stands there sweaty and panting and looking a little freaked.

"Call her. Go to the hospital."

He thinks about this. "Yeah, okay." And he runs back into the game and keeps playing, if you can believe it.

Inggy and I get updates throughout the day. Sherry's home. Her contractions haven't started, so she's lounging on the couch with a diet soda and TV.

Then at seven-thirty I get a text from her. "Shithead won't come to the hospital!!!"

Inggy gets the same text and calls me. "Can you believe him?"

"I know!"

"Maybe we should go," Ing says.

"You think? Okay."

Inggy drives us to the small Catholic hospital by the bay. Out in front there's a statue of the Virgin Mary with her hands outspread. She's standing in the middle of a thorny little garden with a blue spotlight shining on her. I've always liked the Virgin Mary because she's a complicated woman, from what I remember from the stained-glass windows when my grandma took me to church. Even this particular Mary under the blue spotlight looks like she's been around the block and could handle anything. I make the sign of the cross.

We wander for a while and finally wind up in a small maternity waiting area. Sherry's still in labor, so we sit on the plastic couch and I watch an episode of *Police Women of Memphis* while Ing thumbs through a magazine. Things aren't exactly great between us, but they're not terrible either. I buy us Junior Mints from the vending machine.

Ing pokes me. "Can you believe the next time we see Sherry she's gonna be a mom?"

"Freaky."

She shakes her head. "A whole new life is beginning for Sherry right now."

I nod. "So weird to think your life could change instantly."

"Yeah."

I text Sherry: "ing and i r here. did u have it?" It's nearly nine o'clock, and the place is quiet. A couple of nurses walk through, and one looks at us curiously.

My phone rings, making us jump. "It's dead!" Sherry cries.

Ing and I huddle together, the phone between us.

"Dead?" I say, fingering a Junior Mint out of the box.

"Yes!"

"Where are you?" I ask, but she hangs up. Inggy turns pale, if that's possible. "Dead," I mouth.

We stare at each other for the longest time until a young nurse with many tiny braids and a gap between her front teeth stands over us and says, "Girls, you can stay for a few minutes, okay?" She brings us down the hall to Sherry's room.

"It's really dead?" Inggy whispers to the nurse.

"Stillborn, yes," she says.

Sherry is teary, her hair sweaty and pushed off her forehead, and Mrs. Gulari is weeping in the corner, "I can't believe it, I can't believe." She wasn't thrilled about Sherry having the baby, but you'd never know it now.

"Get a grip, Ma," Sherry says. "It's dead," she tells us.

"Why?" Inggy says, and blushes. "I mean, how?"

"They don't know. Stillborn. Do you guys think I should see it?"

I ask, "Was it a—"

"Girl." Sherry swipes her eye with the sheet and smears eyeliner across it. "I didn't really want it, but still . . . I have the worst luck, don't I?" She smiles and bursts into tears, which gets Mrs. Gulari rocking and wailing louder. "I can see her if I want. They think I should. I don't know." She looks at us with big wet eyes. Inggy sits beside her and holds her hand. "It's that bastard Tony's fault. His genes are all screwed up. He drinks too much beer. Eats too many hot dogs. Man, it's no good." She sniffles.

"Geez, Sherry." I sit on the bed. "I'm so sorry."

"You think I should see her? The nurses say so, but I don't know. Maybe you guys can take a look and if it's not too bad I'll take a look. Ma doesn't want to." Mrs. Gulari shakes her head and makes the sign of the cross.

I nod. "I'll go see her."

When the nurse comes back in the room Sherry says, "My friend here is going to take a look for me." But the nurse says no, shaking her little braids, and goes on and on about how Sherry should see the baby, that it helps with the healing process, but Sherry just looks at her, glazed. "Please," she whimpers, a tear running down her cheek. "Can my friend look first, and then I will."

The nurse sizes me up. "You're eighteen?" she asks.

"I am," I lie.

"Just for a minute," she finally says.

I nod and follow her. "How did it happen?"

She shrugs. "These things happen sometimes. Congenital, maybe." And again she talks about how we should encourage Sherry to see the baby, how it'll help her deal with this.

She brings me into a small room where the baby's lying wrapped in a blanket in a plastic crib. She's the only baby in the room because she's dead, which makes me feel a little shaky. I get cold feet for a sec but then step up and look at the little thing. It's so weird. She's beautiful and could be perfectly asleep except for being so still, which really dawns on me the more I stare at her. She has eyelashes and soft hair poking out of the edge of the blanket. "What happened?" I whisper to her.

Someone opens the door and the nurse turns away for a few seconds. I want to touch her, see that she's real. I reach into the blanket's fold and take out her hand, her hand with five little fingers and teeny fingernails. She's not cold, not exactly, which is what I would have thought. I hold her hand for a second, and my heart is breaking a little.

This might be the most grown-up thing that's ever happened to me, and I don't like it. I wish I could rewind the last ten minutes and tell Sherry no. Now I'll always know this baby. I don't want to know her.

"Okay." The nurse comes to my side.

I say something dumb then. "Could you maybe be wrong? Could she be not quite dead?"

She sorta smiles and tilts her head. "It does seem like she's sleeping, the sweet thing."

I walk down the hall with the nurse, feeling dazed. When Mossy was just a baby and I babysat, I'd carry him around in his little seat, even taking him into the bathroom with me because he was so little. He would watch me closely, drinking me in with his big eyes. Even though I was only eight, and he was so small in his feety pjs, I could see that he was already himself, that he was already a little person, just like I could see that Sherry's baby was already inside there, even if she wasn't going to get a chance to come out.

"Just another minute or two," the nurse says to me outside Sherry's room.

When I go back in Sherry looks at me closely. "Tell me," she whispers.

"You don't want to see her."

"I don't?" she asks. Her face morphs from relief to shock and back to dazed.

I shake my head. She can't have that picture in her

head. Of that perfect baby. That glimpse of what might have been. She just can't.

"Okay, thank you, Angel," she says after a minute. "I'm going to name her Angel the second." We sort of laugh. "Well, Giavanna Angel Gulari." She swings her legs out of bed. "Okay, I'm going home." She peeks at the clock. "*Millionaire Matchmaker* is coming on." The nurse, lingering in the doorway, hustles her back to bed and tries again with the healing stuff, but Sherry just shakes her head.

When Ing and I leave, Mrs. Gulari is sitting at Sherry's side holding her hand.

We walk through the hospital, which is quiet except for an occasional ding or beep. "That's the worst thing that's ever happened to me," Inggy says.

I nod. "Me too, kinda."

"What was she like?" Inggy says, touching me.

I really want to tell her, I do, but it just might get back around to Sherry if I tell anybody at all. Not that Inggy would blab, but it might be too hard to hold in. There are so many secrets between us now and that was never what I wanted. I wonder how it happened. "You don't want to know. Really, Ing."

"Oh! Was it terrible?"

"No, no," I say, pushing through the lobby doors into the night dark. "Please, Ing."

She puts an arm around me. "I love you, Angel."

"I love you too." It's that kind of night, and my heart is

still breaking. Outside, the Virgin Mary's arms are still open and I look at her calm face and think *Why?* "I can't go home yet."

"You'll sleep over." So we go to her house, and I change into one of her nightshirts and borrow a toothbrush. I climb into a twin bed, with the dust ruffle, and feel safe. Inggy sits at her desk gathering her books and homework for the morning. Then she clicks off the light and kneels by my side. "You're so brave, Angel. I wish I was more like you."

"You do?" I say, surprised.

"Yeah."

"You have so much more than me," I tell her. She leans her head against the mattress and I touch her fine, silky hair. "Ing, what's going to happen to us?"

"You always ask me, you know that?"

"I do?"

"Yup." I can hear a smile in her voice.

"Remember," I whisper, "how tonight you said Sherry would become a mom and her life would change forever? Will anything happen to change us forever?"

"We'll always be friends," she says.

"Promise me," I say.

"I promise. You're my very best friend." And nothing about tonight feels disingenuous at all. She kisses my forehead and climbs into the other twin.

chapter 18

Life goes on. Funny and sad how that is. At first, Ing and I talk about that weird black-magic night almost to remind ourselves that it really happened. Then we don't talk about it at all. Nobody else does either. It's almost unreal. There was Sherry's huge stomach, then there was a baby for a half a second and then—poof—she was gone. Sherry asks us to come to the funeral, a mini funeral with Sherry and some of her family, but I say I'm sick. Inggy goes to the cemetery and tells me the coffin is tiny and Sherry still looks glazed and hasn't washed her hair in days. And apparently it costs too much to get *Giavanna Angel Gulari* etched on the gravestone, plus there isn't much room with Sherry's great-grandparents already on there, so they settle for *Gia Gulari*, but Sherry says she'll always be Giavanna Angel Gulari. I probably should have gone, but I just couldn't.

• • •

I eat pizza at Fat Sal's with Danny from 7-Eleven. We talk about fishing and school and how much we both love Boar's Head pastrami. Nothing too scintillating, but it's an okay date and the slices are perfectly cheesy. After, he asks me to come over and a watch a movie, and I say why not.

His place, a little apartment over someone's garage, is pretty depressing, I have to admit, but he doesn't seem to mind. He gets us beers from a mini fridge, and we sit on his sagging couch, practically on top of each other, the couch pulling us toward the center, and watch an action adventure. About ten minutes into the movie he says, "You like this?"

I shrug, a little bored. "What do you want to do, then?" I ask.

He's still for a minute and then lies down on the mattress on the floor. It's covered in light green sheets and a gold plaid blanket. He looks up at me. I take in the skanky apartment and say, "I don't know."

"Okay," he says. I join him on the mattress and we talk for a while, staring up at the ceiling. Then out of the blue he asks if a candle would be nice.

"Sure," I say. He lights two small candles and flips off the light, and the overall mood is definitely improved. We fool around, but it's not exactly an adventure.

● ● ●

After I get home I can't sleep, so I wander over to the House for a snack. It's almost two a.m., and TB's in the kitchen baking a pie. I wave.

"My insomniac friend. Hello there. Couldn't sleep?"

I shake my head.

"I'm making comfort food. Even your mom's not feeling well. And poor Mossy. The kid's been upchucking."

"Bart, no one says *upchuck*." I roll a piece of leftover piecrust in my hand.

"What do you kids say? *Barf?*"

"How about *blow chunks*. Poor Mossy."

"He'll be okay." He sweeps apple peels into the garbage. "So your mother likes this banker, it seems."

"As much as she likes anyone."

He smiles a knowing smile.

"My mother's not gonna change, I don't think," I tell him. "Don't you want something more, Bart?"

He sighs. "I'm a dummy, I know."

"Aw, Bart." I rub his back, and his eyes fill with tears.

"That pie's going to be done in twenty minutes. Have yourself a hot slice with a scoop of ice cream."

"It smells amazing."

He lies on the couch under a quilt, and I head upstairs to check on everyone. Mom's buried under the covers, Mossy's flat on his back breathing through his nose and making fluty noises, and Mimi's in a little heap on a nest of pillows. She flutters her eyes.

In the bathroom I look in the mirror, and there I am. Sleepy Mimi shuffles toward me and leans in the doorway with a drippy nose. She climbs up on the sink and wraps her arms around me as we gaze into the mirror. She's still inside a dream, her hair rumpled and her face smooth and still. Everything is yet to happen to her. I'm jealous.

A few nights later, my bedroom light snaps on. "So it was stupid," Cork says, sitting on the edge of my mattress.

"What! Get out!" I shield my eyes from the light.

"I have to tell you."

I'm tired these days and must have left the back door unlocked, because he is where I least want him: sitting on my mattress. Now the light is shining in my eyes and he's shaking my arm. "Please," he says.

"Get off." I shove him and pull the covers up to my chin.

He makes himself comfortable on the floor. "Just listen. She was kinda wasted. Happy wasted. She's sipping a mojito, dancing around the kitchen to Aretha Franklin. The back door's open, and I ask if I can have a snack. 'Eat up,' she says. I take a beer from the fridge and she's cool with that, I guess. To help her out, I follow her around the living room with a trash bag while she grabs up the dirty plates and napkins. She's funny, your mom."

"I'm warning you," I say.

"It just kinda happened."

"Not another word."

"You have to admit it's kinda funny." I scramble to the edge of the bed and kick him in the chest. He lets himself fall back onto the rug and a slow smile spreads over his face. "I was just thinking how no one wants to make out with my mom. Or Inggy's mom. Or most anyone's mom. But your mom is . . ."

"Ass-wipe! She's my *mother*."

"I have a theory—"

"Tell me and I'll have to kill you."

"Okay. I'll stop. But it wasn't like kissing a mom."

"I swear—"

He sits up, and his face becomes serious. "That's why I came to say sorry. I feel like I cheated on you."

"You totally did," I say. "That and more."

"Can we forget it? I don't want your mother. Obviously. I want to go back to how it was."

I shake my head, but he climbs on the bed and puts his arms around me and his warm lips against my forehead. "I'm sorry," he whispers.

"No." I duck under his arm and push him off.

"It was just a kiss, Angel. Come on."

"What about Inggy?"

"What about her?"

"Who else have you been with?"

"Who else have *you* been with?"

I shrug. "I'm free."

"I love Inggy." He picks up my sneaker and whips it around in a circle by the shoelace. "There's something I want to tell you."

"Make it good."

"See, I like that answer. That's why I like you."

"Let me tell *you* something. I feel like I don't know you anymore. . . ."

"Are you gonna let me talk?"

"You've been with other girls, right? Tell the truth."

He sighs.

"Tell me, Cork."

"You know what? Inggy doesn't have secrets yet. I used to think it's not in her DNA, but I was wrong. She just hasn't done anything *yet*. She will. And there may have been a minor episode with a turd named Jeffrey. She may have kissed the turd. I don't know. Anyway, my point is everybody does something at some point."

"Everybody?" I say.

"Everybody." He lies on the rug and puts his arms behind his head, satisfied.

Maybe that's right, but I don't know. I just don't know. I think of my dad, Joey, Inggy, my grandma, old Mrs. B who works in the sub shop. . . .

Cork stretches out and yawns. "We've already dirtied it up, Angel."

"What does that mean?"

He reaches an arm out to me. "I really like you. I miss you."

"You're such an ass-wipe, kissing my mother." I take his hand and let him pull me off the bed.

"Okay, we can stop," he whispers. "If you want to, we'll stop."

"Let's stop."

He kisses me nicely on the lips and smooths his hands over my hair. I let my eyes close for a sec. "And what do you mean you don't know me anymore?" he says. "What would Inggy think of you if she knew?"

"Okay, shut up."

"Why the attitude with me?" he whispers. "Huh? Aren't we in this together?"

"You made out with my mom, idiot!"

"I'm a total idiot." He hugs me, presses his lips against my ear, and I feel him smile. "But you could just give me a blow job for old times' sake."

I shove him. "Yeah, because I can't think of anything else I'd rather do." I mean, really.

"Kidding, sorry." He stands and lifts me to my feet. We hug and sway from side to side. "I don't want to miss you, Angel."

"Tough."

"You smell delicious."

"Oh I do, do I?"

"Spicy. You smell spicy." He puts his lips on my neck.

"And warm." He gives me a tiny lick. "And wet." He runs his hands over my ass in my nightie. "You are the sexiest girl I know. Why are you so sexy?"

"I can't help it." I let him put a hand under my nightie. Once more, just once or twice more.

winter

chapter 19

It's been raining for days, and the wintry sky hangs low over the town. I ride my bike through the streets, which are empty and slick with puddles, and stare at the posters of four smiling girls in the store windows. There we are—me, Inggy, Carmella, and Alyssa—Miss Merry Christmas nominees—next to pizzas, subs, postage stamps, and interest rates, waiting for the town to crown a winner. I park under a streetlamp and stare at the picture of me next to the 20% OFF sign in Stanley's Casuals. It's pretty decent, not like I must look now—a girl in the rain with her hair plastered to her head.

I know it's dumb and it embarrasses me to admit it, but I really want to win, want to see what winning might do for me. I picture myself riding on top of the float, waving my hand, wearing the crown . . . *And here it begins.*

But as I look at the picture of Inggy, I know she'll win. She seems destined. She's not looking at the camera and has a soft smile, the wind gently lifting her white hair. Her eyes are very blue.

But still. Anything is possible, and it's not just about the pictures. I stare at us a little longer, the light rain soaking me good. Carmella is dark and glossy, a bit mysterious, with her head cocked flirtatiously and a no-teeth smile. Alyssa looks sweet, a tiny dark star of a girl with full lips. Me—I have a full-on smile, my curls falling beneath my shoulders, my eyes sparkling like I'm thinking of something good.

When I get back to the House, I towel myself off and snuggle on the couch with Mimi, who's doing long division problems. She chucks her notebook to the floor and whispers, "You're going to be Miss Merry Christmas."

"Yeah, maybe."

"You're the prettiest." Her teeth are small and white, her eyes all dark pupils. She lays her head in the crook of my arm and motions for me to bring my ear close. I lean down and she tells me how she and some of her older friends, girls in the fifth and sixth grades, have gone to every store on the strip and voted for me, filling out a white slip and dropping it into the box beneath our pictures. "I disguised my handwriting," she says. "Don't worry."

A little later I dash over in the cold to my house. Someone rounds the corner by the back steps. Sherry.

"Hey," she calls. "Good timing."

"What's up?" I hug myself.

"Oh, nothing." We go inside and plop down on the couch. I'm a little worried about Cork showing up, but that's easy enough to explain, really. Mostly I'm wondering what she wants. I feel uncomfortable around her, even though I know I shouldn't. She looks at me with big eyes like she's expecting *me* to say something. "You have a Coke or something?"

"Sure." I get it, hoping she's not planning on staying long enough to drink the whole can. She pops it open, takes a sip, and sort of smiles at me. "You all right?" I ask. She's almost back to normal except for her face, which still looks a bit dazed, like she's trying to listen to two conversations at once.

She nods. "Nobody ever talks about it, Angel. Isn't that weird?"

I pat her hand. "No one wants to make you feel bad, probably."

"Well . . . ," she says, picking at the stitching on the couch pillow. "Your picture looks nice. I saw it in the window of Sundae Times." She takes an elastic out of her bag and sloppily pulls her hair back. "Inggy'll probably win, but I really think you have a shot, you know."

I shrug. "Thanks."

She pulls her bag close and rummages through it and takes out a tiny photo. "This is me when I was like a couple hours old. Well, it's either me or my brother, because apparently we were exactly alike." It's faded, but a small face and nose and sweep of hair are there.

"Oh," I say, not wanting to take it, but she hands it to me.

"So, um, was she a freak?" she asks.

I shake my head.

"You can tell me."

"She wasn't a freak."

"She had like ten fingers and toes? A regular head and everything?"

"Totally regular."

"But don't you turn a weird color when you croak?"

"She was, you know, normal color."

"Oh," Sherry says, and my heart starts beating fast. "So, regular, you would say?"

I nod.

There's a knock on the back door. "Come in," I shout. Christ, Cork. But it's Kipper. His eyes bounce from me to Sherry.

"Kipper," Sherry says. She looks at me, surprised.

"We've been dancing," I say. "The fox-trot. We practice."

"Angel's pretty good," he jumps in.

Sherry takes the photo out of my hand and looks at it.

"How's it going, Sherry?" he asks.

"That's nice of you to ask," she says stiffly. "Because nobody does. Nobody wants to remember about my baby. . . ."

"I'm sorry," Kipper squeaks. "It's just—"

"It wouldn't kill anybody to remember," she says, standing. "So I guess you're gonna dance, huh?" She picks up her bag and looks at me, wanting to say something else, I think, but I'm kinda glad she doesn't.

"Here, take the Coke." I fix her ponytail and give her a pat on the back.

When I close the door behind her, Kipper says, "Weird."

"What are you doing here?"

"Well." He blushes. "I just wanted to see you and tell you I voted for you."

"You can't just come over."

"I know. I won't." Honestly, he looks a bit crushed.

"But thanks." I touch his arm. "For the vote."

"I just wish sometimes I could get to decide when we can . . . be together."

"We can't be together."

He stares at me unhappily.

"It was just that one time. Those two times."

He keeps staring at me, looking unhappy and super-skinny, I have to say. "You're not very nice to me, you know."

I put my hands on my hips. "I think I'm very nice to you, Kipper. You wanted to get laid, and I helped you out."

"I know. But I like you. A lot."

"Well, I like you too."

"Yeah, yeah, you like me. . . ."

"Come here. Let's dance."

"No, I'll go." He walks to the door and turns back. "Sherry's kind of nutty, isn't she? I mean, who can forget. . . ."

"I know!"

"You okay?" Kipper asks. I nod. He steps out into the cold and zips his jacket all the way to his chin. "Just know," he says as the wind lifts his hair, "that out here in the universe is a boy who adores you. Lest you forget."

"Bye," I say. I lean against the door, trying to think things through. What must it be like for Sherry? Roaming the halls of school, her huge stomach now a small pudge, back to normal more or less, but babyless, so maybe not so normal after all. And that little faded picture. Oh! Why did she come? If she wanted to know, why didn't she look for herself? I thought I did her a favor. I thought I did Kipper a favor too. So much for helping out!

Maybe Sherry should have looked. It was her baby. Her flesh and blood . . .

There's a tap on the door. Oh my God, not Kipper again. I swing around but it's Cork, hood up, looking at me. I let him in.

chapter 20

I'm staring into the little mirror in my locker, putting on lip gloss, when Sherry comes up. "So," she says. "She was totally regular?"

"Yeah." I finger off the goo below my lip line.

"Well . . . how come if she was like totally regular you told me not to look?"

"I . . . I don't know." I sneak a look at her.

"She wasn't a freak?"

"No. Definitely not."

"So why didn't you think I should look?"

I shut my locker and the metal click echoes down the hall. "She was dead!" I whisper. "It would have been so hard for you."

She nods and stares off into space. "I'm glad she wasn't botched up, you know. Like a little freak. That's what I thought. The nurse goes to me, 'She's beautiful,' but you know they probably think little freaks are beautiful. They're very scientific about the whole thing."

"Yeah."

"Yeah." She looks down the hall but doesn't move.

"Well, some guy is interviewing us for the *Ocean Gazette*." I grab my bag and point to the gym.

"For real?"

"Yeah. 'Cause of the contest."

"You live the life, Angel." Sherry smiles. "Okay then." But she stays right where she is, and as I'm waiting for her to get a move on I can't help but picture the baby again.

"Okay." I put my arms around her and give her a hug, but she stays sorta limp. Then I hurry into the gym.

We're supposed to have cheerleading practice because basketball season just started and our pyramid seriously needs work, but seeing how the newspaper guy is interviewing me, Inggy, Carmella, and Alyssa and we're half the squad, practice isn't happening.

The guy has cool hair—super-curly, and he's grown it out into a kickin' 'fro, but I have to say, he has an oily nose. "So," he says to me as I join the group. "I was just asking how a Miss Merry Christmas nominee spends her day, her week."

We give G-rated answers to his boring question, but he keeps circling back to Inggy and her many projects—her weekend in DC, her Career Spotlight column in the school newspaper and the careers she's highlighting in the recent issue: dog breeder and phlebotomist. Can you believe there's such a long-winded name for a person who draws blood? I mean, really. Eventually he remembers there are three others girls here. "Is this simply a beauty contest or is it more?" he asks us.

"Who cares," Carmella says.

"It seems like a beauty contest to me," I say.

"Well, I have to confess that Miss Merry Christmas doesn't exactly *do* anything," Ing says. "She's a local institution, but she doesn't exactly have a mission."

"Should she?" he asks, which you can tell he thinks is a deep question but for us is only a conversation stopper.

"The winner gets a hundred dollars," Carmella says.

"What would you do with the money?" he asks.

"You know the Toys for Tots drive at the savings and loan? I would spend some of the money on toys . . . for the tots."

Inggy and I smile at each other.

"I'd keep it," Alyssa chimes in. "Look, I'll be honest. I have college to think about. I'd put it in my savings account."

He looks at me and Inggy. "Half for charity, half for my college fund," she says.

"I'll need to give it some thought," I say. "The exact breakdown."

And then he asks us what we think we'll do with our lives.

"I'm going to Rutgers, maybe," Carmella says. "To study broadcasting. I'd be good on TV. Or maybe I'll be a makeup artist."

"Journalism. Most likely," Inggy says.

Alyssa smiles. "Teach elementary school. I love children."

"Well, I'm not sure." I don't meet anyone's eyes. "Maybe public relations or something."

Then he's asking us about colleges, where we applied, and I stay quiet, which is not a problem because it turns out he went to Syracuse, so he and Inggy get into a happy little conversation about that. Carmella roots around in her bag for a cigarette. "Are we done here?" she asks.

The guy sort of nods and keeps on talking to Inggy while Alyssa stares on, waiting for a chance to spring. Carmella and I wander outside and lean against the building. It's a gorgeous day, mild and sunny for December, and I tip my head up to the sun. She looks around slyly before lighting up and taking a deep drag.

"Can I have one?" I ask.

"Seriously?"

I'm totally serious, which shocks me a little.

"Think about it. One puff and you're a smoker again."

"I won't be a smoker again."

She hands me a cigarette with a scolding look.

"You got a match?" I ask.

"You want me to smoke it for you too?" She digs in her amazing bag and finds a pack of matches from Lucky Louie's Arcade. "God, that was highly annoying, wasn't it?"

"Yup. But Toys for Tots. Good one."

"I know, right?" She spots Joey talking to the coach

over by the field and quickly grinds out the cigarette. "Jesus. He's everywhere." She ducks around the side of the building.

I love looking at Joey's back. I seriously do. He has such a sturdy back. Wide shoulders. His jacket hangs off him easily. How good it must feel to be him. Well, I don't want him or anyone else seeing me with a cigarette, so I wander underneath the bleachers and contemplate lighting up.

I could just take a drag. Just one puff. But I bet I'll want more than one puff, and then what if I do buy a pack? Carmella's right. I sniff the cigarette. Maybe one little puff. I light the match and that gives me some satisfaction, the flame catching fire, the little sizzle. I blow it out, though, and toss the cigarette in a muddy puddle before I change my mind. Then I hear my name, so I walk under the bleachers toward two asses and two pairs of legs. It's Kipper and this kid Adam Wasserstein, who plays some instrument in the marching band, I think. He's an intense guy who always has a couple of big boily pimples on his forehead.

"I know," Kipper says. "I'm not stupid. We really are friends, though."

"High school bites. Fortunately there's only seven months left. Then I'm home free, off to Princeton and the rest of my life, where I plan on making six figures and getting laid often. I'll have the house, the BMW M3 convertible, the wife and kids, eventually. But first I spend college and my twenties indulging in immoderate promiscuity and the consumption of libations. But Angel Cassonetti. She'll be knocked up or dinging a cash register somewhere."

"You bitter man," Kipper says.

"Of course I'm bitter. Why shouldn't I be bitter? But the joke's on you."

"I think the joke's on you."

"Fuck off," Adam says. "So what's she like, anyway?"

"Listen, dude, sex is more complicated than I thought. It can be tricky, especially with a new person. You have to kinda figure each other out."

"New person? Bullshit. She's the *only* person in your world."

"Well, she's one more than you got."

"Fuck you."

"And how do you know you'll get into Princeton?"

"There are some things I know, like getting laid is only tricky for pussies like you, not for guys with a seven eighty math SAT score."

"Seven eighty!" Kipper squeaks. "Holy crap. I got six ninety. Still very good, but—"

"Not seven eighty."

"So let me get this straight. Your ninety extra points of wizardry, your knowledge of, say, binomial coefficients, is going to help your dick last longer than a Duracell."

"My point is, smart is smart."

"I can see how smart you are," Kipper says, and laughs.

I walk back to the gym. A 780! A nearly perfect score. What would I have gotten if I'd finished, if I hadn't lost heart and had concentrated hard? Could I have gotten a 600? A 500? Is a 500 even decent? Probably not.

Well, I guess Adam Wasserstein won't be casting a vote my way. No matter, I predict his supremely lousy attitude is going to keep him from getting laid for a long time. And I will *so* not be dinging a cash register.

chapter 21

At the end of second period, Myrtle from the office comes on the PA and says, "The mayor's office called. The votes have been tallied, and this year's Miss Merry Christmas is—" My pencil flutters out of my hand. "Ingrid Olofsson."

Then the bell rings and everyone gathers up their stuff and hustles on to their next class. Cork is one of the first out the door, but he looks back at me for a sec. *Oh well*, he seems to say. I take my time getting my stuff, letting the room empty. Of course Inggy wins. I knew that.

Down the hall Cork has an arm around her and she's rolling her eyes. A couple of kids touch her arm as they pass. She doesn't see me, neither does Cork—their heads are tipped together and it looks like they're having a little moment. I hurry to the locker room and hide myself in a stall. I just a need a minute to let it settle, to not have anyone looking at me. I blow my nose. Why does she get everything?

Laughter and footsteps move through the room and out

into the gym. By the time I get to my locker the room is mostly empty. I change quickly as Inggy runs in.

"Hey, Miss Merry Christmas," I say, tying my sneaker.

She leans down and hugs me. "Ack! We should have tied. I want to sit up there with you."

I half smile.

"Get this." She spins open her locker and chucks her gym clothes on the bench. "Cork is into it. Ha ha. I couldn't get away from him just now."

"That is funny," I say.

She peels off her sweater and her little nipples show through her lacy bra. "He's such a weirdo sometimes."

"It's sweet, Inggy."

Her whole face lights up, with winning, I guess, but with Cork too. I hurry into the gym.

"Cassonetti, you're late," Mullen says. "We're dancing today, people, so find a partner pronto."

Kipper comes over and does a little bow before taking my hand. "It's a travesty," he whispers, spinning us in a circle as Mullen gears up the music. "You'll always be my Miss Merry Christmas."

"Cornball," I whisper back.

"I will be as corny as I wish."

"Arms, people. Remember the position." Mullen demonstrates the hold and then grabs Joey and Carmella out of the traveling circle and rearranges them before shoving them back in.

"I told you," Carmella snaps as Kipper and I glide past.

"Cool it," Joey says.

"Feel the music," Mullen yells.

> *Fly me to the moon*
> *Let me play among the stars . . .*

Inggy and Cork are the last ones in. As the music swells, they run toward each other from opposite ends of the gym, right into each other's arms, as if there's nowhere else for them to be.

At midnight I buy Marlboro Lights at 7-Eleven. I ride home and sit on my back steps, huddled in my jacket, and rip open the pack. I sniff a cigarette, stick it in my mouth, and light the match. But then Cork comes around the corner and the wind blows it out. He sits beside me, takes the cigarette from my lips, and lights it. "Head rush," he says, coughing a little. He holds it out to me, but I don't want it now. He takes a drag and blows a thin stream into the cold air, his hand on my knee. When he's done, he flicks it onto the stones, where it glows red. "Come on." He stands and reaches for my hand.

"I don't want to, Cork."

"Huh?"

I shrug.

"'Cause Inggy won?"

"Don't be an ass. I knew she'd win. She knew she'd win."

He sits down again and puts an arm around me. "Sorry."

I laugh. "You're not sorry."

"Well, I'm in a situation here, aren't I? There's my girl-friend and there's you—"

I put my fingers over his mouth. "You should be happy for her. You did everything right today."

"What does that mean?"

I stand and hand him the pack. "I'm gonna take a ride."

"She doesn't know, Angel." He means about us, and I'm pretty sure he's right. He tags along behind me as I walk my bike over the stones. When I get to the street he grabs the handlebar. "What's wrong? She doesn't know. Seriously."

"But we know."

Both Sardone cars are parked out front and it's pretty late, so there's little chance Carmella is here, but still, as I knock on Joey's window I'm expecting her to appear. I have to knock three times. Little knocks, and finally Joey raises the window, looking sleepy, his hair mashed. He's shirtless and shivers when the cold air hits him.

"I don't know why I'm here," I tell him. If you love someone there must be a moment that announces itself and your heart doesn't wonder because it knows the things it knows. My heart hasn't made any announcement, and yet here I am again.

"It's freezing," he says, hugging himself. "Come in. Go to the door."

I shake my head and point at the open window. It seems better, less intrusive, to come through the window, so he opens it wide and I put my arms around him and he hauls me in, banging his arm on the sill.

"Jesus." He rubs it. "You do everything the hard way, don't you?"

"Oh, stop."

He shuts the window and we sit on his bed, which is still warm from him. The lights over the lagoon fill his room with shadows. He sits close to me. "How about some fancy cheese?"

"I thought you were getting fat and all."

"I'm weak. It doesn't stop me."

He trots off to the kitchen and returns with a cutting board of cheese. "Wait'll you taste this gruyère and Camembert. A couple of my regulars."

"Oh, nice," I say, taking a slice of Camembert.

We don't say much at all. We eat slowly, and this is exactly where I want to be.

I read this book once in middle school about a romance, first love for a bubbly girl who was always taking off her glasses each time she had some deep thought. Anyway, when her crush finally kissed her, "love pierced her with joy," and she took off her glasses, of course. I didn't like the book much but I remembered that part—being pierced with joy—because it fits with Cupid and his trusty arrow. I look at Joey's profile. A strong nose, stubble, lashes touching his cheek when he looks down, dark hair falling over his forehead. And I think how can I still not know if I love him when I'm so aware of him, when I'm still coming to his window, when he's kind of alive inside me? But joy isn't exactly what I feel about Joey. Maybe "piercing joy" is the Hallmark version, love moron-style. Quite possibly love is much more complicated.

He puts an arm around me as we eat cheese. "Sorry about Miss Merry Christmas."

"Oh, it's dumb."

"I voted for you, for what that's worth."

"Thanks."

He nods. "I didn't vote for Inggy. Nothing against Inggy."

"Just me and Carmella, huh?" He's quiet and I nudge him. He stays quiet. "Whoa," I say.

"I like my girlfriend, all right. But lately she's pretty pissy. And I don't think Miss Merry Christmas should smoke and have a bad attitude."

I smile. "Because Miss MC is such an important local institution?"

"Come on. I can just see it. She'd be sitting up there, wearing the crown and lighting up and sending me pissy texts. I'm having none of that."

"You're funny."

"I gave her an ultimatum. Stop smoking or I'm not kissing you. She smells like an ashtray."

"What'd she choose?"

"She's still 'deciding' and will 'get back' to me when she makes a decision, which is kinda what I mean about the attitude." He pops a big chunk of gruyère in his mouth. "I feel duplicitous, not voting for her and all, but oh well." He licks a cheese fleck from his finger.

"*Duplicitous.* That's a good word."

"Yeah, Murphy uses it in English lit. I like it." He picks up my hand and holds it. "Anyhow, sorry about the contest. I know you kinda wanted it."

I look up at his sleepy face. "You're a nice guy, Joey."

"Is that why you're here?"

"You mean something to me."

We're quiet for a time, and I rest my head against his bare shoulder.

"What do I mean to you?" he asks.

"Something."

"Something?"

"Something that makes me keep coming back."

He lies back on his pillow with a little sigh, and I curl up beside him and put my palm over his heart and feel it beating there quick and strong, rising up to meet my hand. A boy's heart, I think. The heart is pure. This must be true. If the body and head aren't always, then the heart is. I keep one hand over his heart and the other over mine. They pump hard and fierce to a steady beat.

chapter 22

We're having a bonfire on the beach, and Sherry plops down next to me on the sleeping bag. The fire crackles and spits and for a second smoke blows in our eyes.

"Look at the moon," she says, squinting. "It's blue."

It's a full moon and definitely bluish. "Maybe it means something good."

She takes a sip of beer. "I hope."

"Me too."

"I'm feeling a little better, you know." She tosses the sleeping bag off her legs and stares up at the sky. "I can't go to the parade tomorrow. I got a weekend job at Macy's."

"You did?"

"Yeah. My cousin works in lingerie, supposedly lingerie, but she's always at the sock counter. Go figure. Socks are totally boring. I'll be in luggage. Luggage seems interesting."

"Definitely, plus the store discounts, right?"

"Uh-huh," she says. She lets out a sigh and unzips her

jacket. "I probably would have been a crappy mom, being so young and all. I didn't really want her, you know. Maybe she knew that."

"Well . . . ," I say. "You hadn't met her yet, you know, so it doesn't really count."

She makes a face. "I ate too many potato chips and Diet Cokes. I probably killed her. Babies, you know, they need milk and vegetables and stuff. Plus I used the f-bomb a lot."

"You used to hold your stomach a lot. She must have felt that, your hands around her."

"Yeah?" Sherry shrugs. "I guess I did. . . . That's nice of you to remember, Angel."

The fire's hot and I unwind my scarf. Across the way, Carmella, Kipper, and Inggy are making s'mores. Cork sits nearby drinking a bottle of beer. His eyes find me and keep moving. Joey talks with some of the football players, tipping his head back now and then, laughing.

"Why didn't you tell me to see her?" Sherry whispers.

Kipper holds up a stick with a toasted marshmallow. "Marshmallow, girls? S'more?"

"Messy but scrumptious," Inggy calls, licking her fingers. "Want one?" Sherry and I shake our heads.

"I mean," Sherry whispers, "you said she wasn't a freak, so why did you tell me not to see her?"

I take a deep breath. "I guess I thought she might break your heart."

"Oh." I can feel her eyes on me. "Would it have been so

bad if my heart was broken?" She doesn't say it like she's mad, only wondering.

"There are worse things than a broken heart," I say.

"A broken heart won't kill you."

I turn to her, and she still looks a little dazed, her bangs flung across her forehead. "She was pretty, Sherry."

"Pretty, yeah?"

"Little and pretty."

"Oh," she says softly. "Little and pretty."

"Totally."

"Kinda like that picture I showed you?"

"Kinda."

"I probably should have looked."

I nod.

She sniffs and wipes her nose. "Well, I'm not mad at you, Angel. 'Cause you were caring about my heart and all. But if you ever, like, see one that looks like her you'll tell me, right?"

"I definitely will."

I lie back on the sleeping bag and look up at the sky. By the shoreline I can hear the crash of waves.

"I wish I looked," she says.

"I wish you did too." I look up into her face, her cheeks rosy from the fire, and I hold her hand. "I'm so sorry."

We sit together for a few minutes before she says, "I guess I should go. I'm a working girl now. Try to have fun tomorrow."

"All right."

She lifts herself off the sleeping bag and says her good-byes.

Ing drops down next to me. "What were you two talking about so intensely?"

"I fucked up."

"Tell me."

"Look at the moon, will you."

"Gorgeous." Inggy has static cling from her scarf and some blond hairs float away from her scalp, and she has a marshmallow fleck on the corner of her lip. "Tell me."

So I tell her about Sherry—all the questions, the little photo. And what I saw in the crib that night. The pretty little baby alone in that room, wrapped in a blanket, so still. Inggy hugs her knees and stares into the sand, listening with her whole self. "Sherry should have seen her baby," I whisper.

"What a hard decision. Seriously."

"Now she'll always wonder. I was wrong."

"But you're right. It might have totally broken her heart."

"Giavanna Angel Gulari will always be a blank in her mind, like some paper doll cutout."

Inggy sorta smiles. "No, she won't. Sherry will invent her. And with a name like that she already has personality."

I turn and look at her, my beautiful friend. "That's such a nice thing to say."

"It's kinda true."

I hug her. "I am so sorry, Ing."

She turns to me. "For what?"

"I'm gonna do better. I promise."

She laughs. "You're squeezing too tight. Jesus."

"I'm gonna do a lot better, Inggy." I let her go and stare up at the blue shining moon. Hope and bliss and heartache swell inside me. I want to make myself a promise; it's that kind of night. "Listen. I really *really* don't want to go to school next year. And you know what, I'm not going!"

"Really? No?" She looks disappointed.

"Nope. I'm not going! I wanna work. Maybe I'll move to the city."

"What kind of job will you get?"

"Don't laugh."

"I won't."

"Receptionist." I check her face, and she's listening. "I like to talk. Obviously. I could buzz people in, make them comfy, set up appointments and stuff. It's not much, but I like the idea. I'll look around, learn the ropes. . . . I'll have my own desk . . . my own stapler. I'll be out in the world."

She thinks about this, sifting sand through her long fingers. "You'd be a good receptionist. I can see it."

"I can see it too."

She laughs. "A stapler! Okay, I'm buying you one for graduation."

"A fancy one."

"You got it."

Inggy and I sit on the bed of the float sharing a bag of corn chips. Some official hands her an envelope and inside is a crisp one-hundred-dollar bill. She hikes up her cape and pockets it. Today she's wearing a little pearly eye shadow and some lipstick, and the rhinestone tiara is sparkling on her head. The red velvet cape is too short on her and her jeans and sneakers stick out the bottom. Carmella, Alyssa, and I are wearing white velvet capes.

A folding chair is perched on top of the staircase in the middle of the float. "Come," I say, climbing the staircase because I want to try out the seat and see the view. I sit on the chair, and Inggy parks on the step.

"So what do you think?" she asks.

"Not bad."

The day is cold, crisp, and gray. Seagulls sit on the telephone wires watching us. Carmella and Alyssa hunch together in their billowy white capes and seem to be reading each other's palms. I wonder what they see there.

Behind us are the school's marching band, flag twirlers, a float with gift-wrapped people standing around a Christmas tree, another float with assorted elves. There are honks and toots and mini drumrolls as the band warms up. A baton shoots through the air and plummets into a twirler's hand.

"Places, girls," a fat man from the chamber of commerce

says to us, and I slowly climb down and take my place on the right rear corner of the float. Next to me are Styrofoam stars attached to broom handles.

We creep along to the tune of "We Wish You a Merry Christmas" as people on the sidewalks wave to us. The O's snap pictures and gallop alongside us for a block. Inggy sits on the folding chair, flushed yet pleased, beaming her smile down on her mom and dad. There's nothing to do but wave my arm.

Up ahead I see my mom, TB, and Mossy on the curb. Mom, incognito, wears big dark glasses and a beret. When we get near them Mom takes pictures and my little man waves like mad and reaches into his pocket and holds something up in the air. Oscar the mouse, I'm guessing. "Oscar," I shout up to Inggy, but I don't think she hears me.

Mimi is boycotting the parade, at least that was what she said when I left her this morning, slurping up Froot Loops. When she and Mossy found out I hadn't won they put their arms around me, but it was Mimi who sobbed, huge tears running down her blotchy face, her whole body heaving. Maybe she wanted me to pave the way for her. "You like Inggy, right?" I said.

"Not anymore."

"But I get to ride on the float too."

"So what?" she sobbed.

I hope she'll change her mind, and I keep a lookout for her pom-pommed hat as we roll along. We pass Kipper, sitting on the curb eating an apple, and Cork in front of the hardware store, sitting on bags of fertilizer. Joey stands in front of Fat Sal's, eating a slice.

My phone blips in my back pocket and I reach under my cape. It's a message from Joey—Joey, who hasn't sent me a text since last spring.

"u mean something 2 me 2."

"i am ready," I write back.

But he doesn't reply. Not yet. He's gonna give it a think. And I will too. I'll try harder, Joey. I will. We can surprise ourselves. I make these little wishes and hope they get carried through the crowd to Joey, eating his slice in front of Fat Sal's.

I see my dad, taking a picture. He has Lily on his shoulders and Ginger is holding Abby. The girls blow kisses and so does my dad, and I stare in his direction until after we pass.

Then I see Mimi, hiding behind a mailbox in front of the savings and loan and watching for me. As the float glides toward her she pushes her way into the street. "That's my sister," she shouts, pointing at me. She looks as if she's waiting for something to happen and I almost expect something to happen, but the float coasts on like a cloud though the sky and I lose sight of her pom-pommed hat.

We stop short. I stumble, nearly stepping on Inggy's tiara, which lands by my feet. It's hard to see what's happening, so I climb the little staircase to Inggy, carrying her crown. Up ahead a car has rear-ended a police cruiser, bringing everything to a stop. Inggy inches over and I share the folding chair with her. "You're not crying, Angel, are you?"

"I'm not crying." She slings an arm over my shoulder and pulls the bag of corn chips from under her cape. That's all I want then, to sit beside her, eating chips and looking out over the town.

In front of us, the ladies' auxiliary put down their banner and start yakking. Carmella hides behind a Styrofoam star and lights up. Alyssa gently waves her arm to the crowd, which isn't paying attention.

The air is still and calm and cold. I heard it might snow later tonight, the first snow of the year. It's only supposed to be a light dusting, but I hope it'll be enough to cover the town in a clean sheet of white.

acknowledgments

Bighearted thanks to my excellent team: Tina Bennett, Wendy Lamb, Svetlana Katz, Dana Carey, Colleen Fellingham, Isabel Warren-Lynch, Barbara Perris, Caroline Gertler, Courtney Carbone, Sabrina Ricci, and Tamar Schwartz.

Huge thanks to my friends and readers for advice, support, inspiration, and all forms of goodness: my writing group, the Talls (at 5'7" I was the shrimp)—Sarah Bardin, Melissa Johnson, and Emilie Oyen; also Maggie Carino-Ganias, Shelley Griffin, Nancy Skinner, Mindy Lewis, Irene Bauman, Matt Guarino, Tom Guarino, Suzanne White, and Leah Friedman.

Finally, thanks to all my dance friends for the joy of swing—the perfect antidote to the writer's life. *It don't mean a thing if it ain't got that swing.* . . .

about the author

Beth Ann Bauman is the author of the short-story collection *Beautiful Girls* and the young-adult novel *Rosie and Skate*, which was a *New York Times* Editors' Choice and a *Booklist* Editor's Choice, as well as a *Booklist* Top Ten for Youth in two categories. She lives in New York City but will always be a Jersey girl at heart. Visit her at bethannbauman.com.